First Farm in the Valley: Anna's Story

Also by Anne Pellowski

Winding Valley Farm: Annie's Story
Stairstep Farm: Anna Rose's Story
Willow Wind Farm: Betsy's Story
The Nine Crying Dolls, a Story from Poland

First Farm in the Valley: Anna's Story

BY ANNE PELLOWSKI
pictures by
WENDY WATSON

PHILOMEL BOOKS
New York

Acknowledgments

The author wishes to thank the following for their assistance:

Trempealeau County Courthouse Officers and Staff; the Wisconsin State Historical Library; Rev. Edward Stanek, Sacred Heart Church, Pine Creek; Marie Marazzi and staff of the Genealogical Library, New York Branch, Church of Jesus Christ of Latter Day Saints; Marie Dorsch, Winona County Historical Society; Winona Public Library.

Library of Congress Cataloging in Publication Data
Pellowski, Anne.
First farm in the valley.
Summary: Anna, born in America, longs
to escape the rigors of Wisconsin farm life
to visit the romanticized Poland of her dreams.
[1. Polish Americans—Fiction.   2. Farm life—Fiction.
3. Wisconsin—Fiction]   I. Watson, Wendy, ill.   II. Title.
PZ7.P365Fi   [Fic]   82-5323
ISBN 0-399-20887-9   AACR2

To Victor Pellowski, son of Barney,
and to
Anne Farrell Lipinski, granddaughter of Anna,
with gratitude

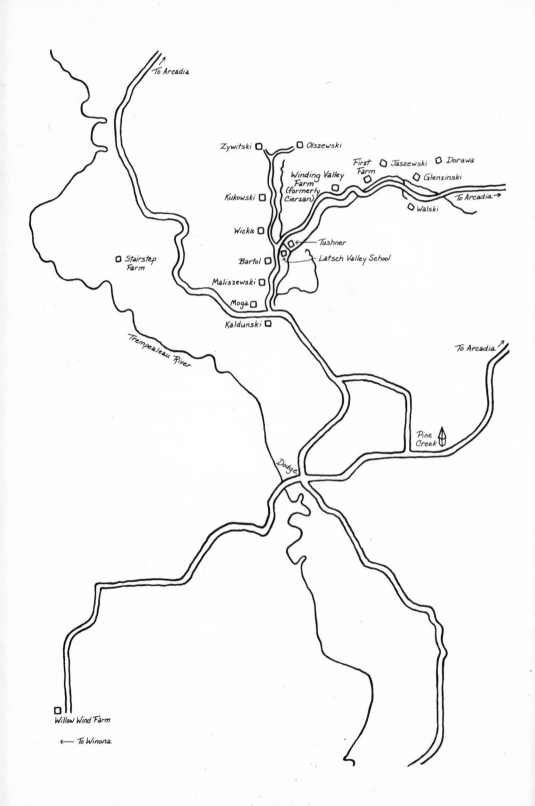

Contents

Anna's Family

Anna was an American, although she did not know it. She was born in Wisconsin, but her family spoke Polish, as did most of the families that lived around her, so she thought of herself as Polish, even though she knew Poland was far, far away.

The valley she lived in was long and winding because the road followed a meandering creek that wove in and out along the edges of the low hills and ravines. Far back in the valley, at a spot where the road and creek turned sharply right, was the farm where Anna's parents had their homestead.

In spring or early summer the road was knee-deep with mud, because the rain and melting snow came rushing down from the hills, settling in low pockets and ruts. Eventually, the water drained off into the creek, or dried in the hot summer sunshine, but for a few months it stayed in the road bed, turning the dirt there into an oozing, squelchy strip of mud.

Father did not like it, because the horses and oxen could hardly pull the wagon or plow through the deep mud. Mother complained because it spattered and splashed on everyone's clothes, making extra work with her washing. But Anna loved it because in the warm days of spring she was allowed to go barefoot again, and one of the first things she did was to go stomping and marching in the slippery, slidy, muddy road. She tried to hold up her skirts so they would not get splashed, but no matter how high she held them, she usually ended up with muddy spots and blotches along the hems of her dress and petticoats.

"Why must you always go fooling around in that mud?" asked Mother crossly.

Anna hung her head in shame. She didn't want to make extra work for Mother, but she couldn't stay away from the mud.

One morning, as she was helping Mother mold the butter that had just been churned, she tried to explain.

"That's why I like it. It's like butter between my toes."

"What is?" Mother looked completely bewildered.

"The mud. It makes my feet and toes feel just like this." With her fist Anna squeezed the lumps of butter to get out all the buttermilk, and it squished and squirted so satisfyingly that even Mother had to agree, with a laugh, that it felt good.

In summer the hot sun dried the mud, and the

turning of heavy wagon wheels and trodding of many oxen and horses' hoofs crushed it into a soft, pale gray powder. Then, walking on the shady parts of the road felt cool and soothing to Anna's bare feet, but when she was forced to pass over the places where the sun beat down all day, she hopped and skipped as fast as she could because the sandy, powdery dirt stung and pinched as it touched the tender skin around her toes.

Pauline and Mary, Anna's two older sisters, did not like going barefoot any more.

"It's babyish," said Mary. She was only nine but considered herself a young lady. Pauline was a year younger and copied everything Mary did.

"All the same, you have to put your shoes aside," insisted Mother. "I don't want you wearing them out. I'm hoping you can both start school next winter, and we can't be buying you new shoes before then. The ones you have must last for another year."

Anna's brothers did not argue about going barefoot. One by one, they shucked off their shoes the moment Mother said it was safe: first, Julian, the baby, who was just learning to walk; then Anton, who was almost four and liked the mud as much as Anna; then seven-year-old Barney; and Franciszek, who at twelve was growing so fast his feet were always too big for his shoes. Even Jacob, who was sixteen and already taller than Father, liked to leave his heavy hobnailed boots by the door and wiggle his toes in freedom as he trudged through the fields or worked in the barn.

In the high bank of the creek, where it made the sharp curve right, was the mouth of a spring. Throughout the year there was a steady flow of cool, sparkly water trickling down from the small hole. In the deep shadows

it looked like a silvery snake coming out of its den. When the snow melted, the snaky trickle became a torrent, carrying everything with it, and filling the creek bed with its angry foam.

"Stay away from the creek for a few days," Father warned the children when it was dangerous.

Above the spring and a little to the side was the old sod house. In winter, Father housed the pigs there to keep them snug and warm. But in summer it stood empty, and sometimes Anna and Pauline played there. It was always cool and they felt it was a nice, secret place to play pretend games.

"Did you really, truly live there?" Anna asked Mother one day. She could hardly imagine Father stooping down to fit in that small, low space.

"We did," Mother assured her. "All by ourselves, the first year: your father, Jacob and I. There wasn't another soul in the whole valley. Then Franciszek was born, and we had a good wheat crop, and your Father earned some money in the lumber mills, so we could put up this house. First we built the front part, and after Pauline was born, we added on the back." Mother looked proudly around her, and Anna followed her glance.

"It is a nice house," said Anna. "Just right for us."

In the long front room was the kitchen, with the stove, a table and benches where they ate, and two rocking chairs with a small table in between, where Mother and Father sat in the evenings. Behind the long room were two bedrooms: one for her parents and one where she and her sisters slept. The boys all slept in the attic overhead, except for Julian. He still slept with Mother and Father.

"I don't see where there's room for anyone else," Anna said to herself one day in August when they heard some surprising news.

All spring and summer that year Father had talked about his sister, Bridget. He had sent money so she could take the ship from Poland to America. Now, word had come that she had arrived in Winona, the city on the Mississippi River, twenty miles away, where Father sold his wheat and did his business.

"I wonder how she'll look after sixteen years?" Father hurried excitedly through breakfast one morning. That day he was going to see her for the first time in all those years.

"She's probably not changed much," said Mother calmly.

But when Father returned late that evening even Mother could not contain her excitement.

"How is she? Did she have a hard time on the crossing? Was the ship as crowded as ours?" She pelted Father with questions.

"She's fine. And she didn't like the trip any more than you did," laughed Father.

"I should think it was even harder. A widow alone with her children," Mother clucked in sympathy.

"Does Aunt Bridget have children?" asked Anna in surprise. She was getting used to the idea of having an aunt, and now, for the first time, she heard that with Aunt Bridget came some children.

"And quite a handful, too," chuckled Father.

"How many *does* she have?" asked Mother. "She didn't make it clear in the letter."

"Well, let me see now. Was it four? No, six! Or maybe there were five." Father scratched his head and then looked sheepishly at Mother. "You know, I never did ask her outright, and there were so many other young ones at the house where she's staying that I couldn't count them myself."

"You're a fine one!" Mother chided him. "So excited about seeing your sister, you forgot all about your nephews and nieces."

"Does that mean they are our cousins?" asked Pauline.

"Yes. Your first cousins. The only ones you have here in America." Mother had a sad look in her eyes as she answered.

"When will we get to see them?" asked Anna.

"Soon," answered Father with a smile.

The New Family

From all sides, Anna could hear the buzzing and pounding sounds of building. On the roof of a small, newly built house, her father was helping their new neighbor, Mr. Olszewski, put row after row of shingles in neat, tight layers. At one of the side walls, Jacob sawed away, cutting out the spaces for windows. Beyond the house, in the direction of their farm, she could see Franciszek, Barney and Pauline helping the older Olszewski children. Using Father's two teams of horses, they were hauling logs from the edge of the woods to a spot where the barn would be.

Mother was stirring something in a large iron pot that sat on three legs over a glowing fire. Mary worked at a stump nearby, cleaning and chopping carrots and dropping them into the pot as soon as they were ready.

Anna's job was to watch her two little brothers, with Susan Olszewski to help her. There was no Mrs. Olszewski. She had died more than a year ago, before the Olszewskis moved to Dodge. They had come from Poland to America at the same time as Father, but had lived in Canada for ten years.

The sun moved higher into the sky, until it was almost overhead. From his perch on the roof, Father squinted up at it.

"Is that soup ready yet?" he called down from the housetop.

"Another few minutes and it will be," answered Mother.

"Then I guess it's time to stop." Slowly he and Mr. Olszewski made their way to the edge of the roof and stepped cautiously down a rough pole ladder. Anna wanted to climb that ladder and go to sit on the top of the house, but she didn't think Father would allow her.

"Come! Time to pray and eat!" Father called loudly.

As soon as they were all standing around the bubbling pot, Father began the Angelus, chanting the words in his deep, mellow voice:

The Angel of the Lord declared unto Mary;

Mother started to sing the response and they all joined in:

And she conceived of the Holy Ghost.

Back and forth went their musical prayer, with Father and Mr. Olszewski starting off each verse and Mother leading the rest in answer. When they had finished Mother gave the soup a last stir and tasted it.

"It will do," she said, and began to ladle big portions into the tin bowls and cups that were waiting on a stump nearby. Father and Mr. Olszewski took their bowls and big chunks of bread and went to sit under the shade of a maple tree that was still covered with thick clumps of golden leaves.

The children followed, balancing their bowls and cups so as not to spill them. Last of all came Mother, carrying her bowl and walking slowly so Julian could keep up with her by clutching her skirt and stumbling alongside.

"Mm, mm!" Father smacked his lips. "Nothing like a good cabbage soup to fill you up."

"There's plenty more," said Mother as she cautiously blew on a spoonful of soup before popping it into Julian's mouth.

Anna dunked her chunk of bread into the soup and then sucked it into her mouth. The soup-soaked bread slid down her throat as smoothly as pudding.

They ate and ate, until the pot was empty. With a satisfied sigh, Father leaned back against the tree trunk. Mr. Olszewski made a move to get up, but Father motioned him back.

"Sit awhile yet. There's only a row or two of shingles left to nail down. And we should have no trouble finishing most of the barn before dark, with all these helpers." He glanced around at all the children.

Mr. Olszewski looked overcome. "I surely do appreciate your help," he said. "It would have taken us till the snow flies to do it on our own."

"We're just so glad to have neighbors in this direction," said Mother. "I won't worry so much when the children take the sheep or cows to pasture back here."

"That's right," thought Anna. "Now we have neighbors on every side of us." To the east lived the Jaszewskis and Glenzinskis and beyond them, the Dorawas. On the south side of the road and creek, lived the Walski family. Father always said: "Yah, that Walski, he knew we had a good place here—he came right on our heels."

Next to the Walskis lived the Tushners. They spoke with an accent, using different words, and Mother had once explained to Anna: "That's because they come from Bohemia."

Last year, the Cierzans had moved onto the farm west of them and Anna had been delighted because Julia Cierzan was the same age as she was, and now she had a

18

friend to play with besides her brothers and sisters.

West of the Cierzans lived the Wickas, the Kukowskis and the Zywitskis.

"Imagine!" exclaimed Father. "You'll be the fourteenth family in the valley. Who would have thought it when I came here twelve years ago, and not a house around, except Mr. Latsch's, at the head of the valley. And even his family was afraid to live here, because he was gone to the war." Father's eyes took on a deep, faraway look as he remembered those days.

Anna could see that he was as happy as Mother about all the new neighbors. But she could also tell that he was proud to have started the first farm in the valley.

Father stood up and stretched.

"A snooze would feel good right about now," he laughed, "but Bridget would never forgive me if I didn't get those shingles on tight. She won't want to have any rain coming into that snug little house. So, I guess it's back to work." He and Mr. Olszewski strolled over to the ladder and climbed up to the roof again.

Anna was confused. "Is Aunt Bridget going to live in this house?" she asked Mother.

"Maybe, in a few months," said Mother with a smile.

"But I thought Father was helping to build it for Mr. Olszewski and *his* family," said Anna, still puzzled.

"It will be for them," said Mother. "But if all goes well, Aunt Bridget will marry Mr. Olszewski and they'll both live here. Then he will be your uncle. Won't that be fine?"

Anna was not sure. Until a few months ago, she had not known that she had any relatives. Now she suddenly had an aunt and some cousins, and before too long she might have an uncle.

"What about Susan and Johnny and the other Olszewskis?" she asked.

"They'll be your cousins, too," explained Mother. "Your cousins by marriage."

Anna was still thinking about her new cousins when Father and Mr. Olszewski finished the roof and moved across the field to work on the log barn. The rest of the family followed, to see if they could help.

Mr. Olszewski looked around and felt in his pockets. Then he turned to Johnny.

"Run back to the house and bring me my bag of nails. I must have left them there somewhere."

"Mine, too," said Father.

"I'll help you look," offered Anna and she skipped after Johnny.

"They're not here," said Johnny after he had circled the house inside and out.

"I didn't see them either." Anna stared at the tall ladder still propped against the roof. "Do you suppose they left them up there?"

"Maybe," said Johnny, but he made no move toward the ladder.

"I'll climb up and look," said Anna, but she, too, continued standing where she was.

"You wouldn't dare!"

"Yes, I would!" Anna took a few steps in the direction of the ladder.

"Better let me do it," said Johnny as he tried to move ahead of Anna.

"I said it first so I'm going up first," insisted Anna.

"Well, go on then!" Johnny looked almost relieved.

Grasping the second rung, Anna started to climb up the ladder while Johnny steadied it. She did not look down until she came to the top rung. Her knees trembled and almost gave way. Johnny seemed so far away! Then she glanced sideways in the direction of a grove of trees growing on the north side of the house.

"I'm level with the treetops," she gloated. When she looked straight ahead, the dizzy feeling disappeared.

"Hurry up!" called Johnny. "Can you see if they're up there?"

Anna scanned the side of the roof. Row upon row of fresh shingles overlapped each other, neatly and smoothly. A few feet below the roof ridge was a long plank, resting on small blocks of wood that had been nailed to the beams, through the shingles. The plank had allowed the men to work safely. It would have caught them if their feet started to slip down on the smooth shingles. Leading up to the plank on the side of the roof right above the ladder were stepping blocks of wood, also nailed down tight. Mr. Olszewski had left the plank and the blocks there because he still had to finish off the stovepipe hole.

"The nail bags must be on the plank," Anna called to Johnny. "I'm going up to see."

"I don't think you should. Let me come up and do it."

Anna paid no attention to his words, but inched her way upward, grasping the higher block with her hands and curling her toes around the lower one. At last she was high enough to peer over the edge of the plank. There, tucked way back and almost falling into the narrow space between the roof and the back of the plank, were the nail bags.

She could have reached them by taking one more step, but now that she was so close to the ridge pole, she wanted to sit astride it. By standing on the plank and

21

stretching upward with her stomach flat against the roof, she could just manage to see over the top.

"I'm going up there," she announced, but not too loudly.

"What did you say?" Johnny called up.

Without answering, Anna swung herself up, placed one leg on the other side and then straightened the upper part of her body. She was sitting on top of the world! Ahead of her were rolling fields and ravines, spread out like Indian blankets with their alternating shades of browns and grays. On the north were the poplar and maple trees gently shaking their red and golden leaves like girls with bouncing curls. When she looked south, Anna was so startled she almost lost her balance. There, peeking out from the woods more than a mile away, were their own barn and house. The world certainly looked different from so high up!

"Why, I'm seeing it the way birds do," she thought.

"What's taking you so long?" growled Johnny.

"I'm coming," answered Anna. She would have liked to stay up there all afternoon, but Father and Mr. Olszewski needed the nails. Slowly, carefully, she lowered herself to the plank, picked up the two bags of nails in one hand and then worked her way downward on the blocks toward the ladder. When she came to the last two blocks, she hung on to the upper one, but let her feet slide loose from the lower. With her toes she felt for the ladder, but all they encountered was empty space.

"Where's the ladder?" she shrieked. Would Johnny have been so mean as to take it away?

"A little to your left," shouted Johnny.

At last her toes touched the first rung and she clambered down, handing the nail bags to Johnny as soon as she could reach down to him. Hardly had she stepped off the ladder when Franciszek came running around the corner of the house.

"Father thinks he left the nails on the . . ." Franciszek's voice trailed as he saw them in Johnny's hand. "So you found them? Weren't you scared to go up and get them?"

Anna held her breath.

"They weren't so hard to get down," said Johnny and then he grinned at Anna. He wasn't going to tell.

Then and there, Anna decided she'd like having him as a cousin.

The rest of autumn flew by. Father visited Aunt Bridget again, in Winona, and this time Mother went with him.

"Did you see her children?" asked Anna. "How many does she have?"

"Yes," laughed Mother. "She has five of them. Four boys and a girl. That will be quite a family when she marries Mr. Olszewski."

Slowly Anna counted on her fingers.

"Eleven children!" she exclaimed. "More than in our family. Where will they all sleep?" She pictured in her mind the small house they had helped to build. It didn't seem big enough for thirteen persons.

"They'll fit in," answered Mother calmly. "Mary Olszewski is getting married soon and Joe is working in Winona. Bridget's oldest boy will probably go off, too, looking for work. They'll have a lot more room than we had in the sod house."

Suddenly Anna had another thought.

"Will there be a wedding?" she asked. Last summer, they had all gone to a wedding in Dodge, and she had watched the dancing until she had fallen asleep. From what she had seen, she liked weddings.

"Yes," laughed Mother. "There will probably be a wedding, right after Christmas. Nothing fancy, but still, a wedding."

Wedding Day

On the second day of February, Anna's family got dressed in their best clothes. Mother brought out her special velvet hood, embroidered in silver and gold, that she had worn on her own wedding day in Poland many years ago. She wrapped the hood around her head and held it in place with a square silk shawl.

The children bundled up in coats and shawls and scarves and mittens. Mother handed each of them a hot baked potato, to keep their hands warm, and they ran outside and jumped onto the wagon box that sat on runners in front of the house. Father and Jacob snapped into place the harnesses of Lord and Lady, their best team, and then they were off to Pine Creek, where Anna

25

and her brothers and sisters would meet their Aunt Bridget and their cousins for the first time.

"What will they be like, I wonder?" Anna whispered to Pauline.

"We'll soon see," she answered.

The February morning was cold, crisp and sunny. The jingling of the horses' bells spread through the clean air, surrounding the sled with the same repeated pattern of tinkly notes, over and over again. In between the notes came the accents of the horses' hoofs as they bit into the crunchy snow.

Jingle, jangle! Crunch, scrunch! Jingle, jangle! Crunch, scrunch!

"My ears are ringing!" cried Anna. On such cold, clear days every sound seemed louder and sharper.

As soon as they turned the corner at the Broms' farm, just at the edge of Pine Creek, Anna could see the unfinished steeple of the new church. She could still remember the big celebration last year, when Father and all the other men had completed the roof on the main part of the church. But the steeple stuck up in the air like a small, unfinished house that the wind had blown to the church roof. Some day a bell would be hung there.

Father drove almost to the church door and they jumped out of the wagon box.

"Take the team to the shed," he said, handing the reins to Jacob.

When they entered the church, they saw the Olszewskis sitting on one side and Aunt Bridget and her family on the other. Father and Mother genuflected and took the pew behind Aunt Bridget. The children filed in behind them. As if on signal, Father Snigourski stepped out from the sacristy and began the wedding ceremony.

He hurried as much as he could, for it was icy cold in the church. In less than an hour Aunt Bridget and Mr. Olszewski had exchanged vows, received the priest's blessing and were standing at the back of the church, shaking hands with Mother and Father.

The Olszewski children stood to one side and looked nervously at Aunt Bridget's children, who stared right back. Anna and her brothers and sisters silently eyed all their cousins: the ones from Poland that they had never met before, and their new cousins by marriage.

"Well, now," said Mr. Olszewski, rubbing his hands together. "We need something to warm us up in such freezing weather. Why don't we all head for our house? I understand Mrs. Cierzan has some tasty food and drink, just waiting for us to get back."

"I guess it would be better for everyone to get acquainted at the house," agreed Father. "Bring the sled back around, Jake, so your mother doesn't have to walk through all that deep snow."

Each family stood in a little clump, not saying much, until the older boys drove up with two sleds and a fine sleigh pulled by a team of bay horses.

"Is that what you came in, Bridget?" Father looked at the sleigh in surprise.

"Yes, we rented it at the livery stables in Winona. Joe will take it back this afternoon. He had to return somehow, because they expect him back at the lumberyard tomorrow, so we thought this would be best." Aunt Bridget blushed a little. She didn't want them to think she had rented the fancy sleigh for show.

Like a small parade, the sleigh and two sleds lined up and set off.

"My potato is cold," complained Anna.

"Don't throw it away," warned Mother. "We'll skin them and fry them up after we get there. I'm sure we'll need all the food we can scrape up. If your hands are cold, sit on them."

A half-hour later they drove into the Olszewski farmyard. The board walls of the new house were no longer creamy white, as they had been right after they were put up, but had weathered to a pale gray from all the autumn rains and winter snows.

Mr. Olszewski opened the door and they all stomped their feet to get rid of the snow before stepping into the house. By the stove stood Mrs. Cierzan, stirring something in a large pot.

"I thought a hot bowl of *zocerka* would be just right to start with, to warm your insides," she announced.

"How good it smells!" exclaimed Mother. "Can I help you dish it up?" Mrs. Cierzan nodded and she and Mother ladled the *zocerka* into bowls and cups. There were not enough chairs or benches, so everyone stood around, sipping the thick, creamy soup with its chunks of crinkly egg dumplings.

"That should hold you until I get the dinner served," Mrs. Cierzan said with a satisfied smile. "We'll have to eat in two batches. There's not enough room at the table."

"Good! That will give the children a chance to get to know each other while they wait," said Father. "But first, I want you to come up and meet your aunt properly."

One by one they approached Aunt Bridget as Father told her their names. She shook hands with Jacob and Franciszek, but when Mary, Pauline, Barney and Anna stepped up shyly, she kissed them on both cheeks. Anna had never been kissed before like that, by someone she hardly knew. It felt strange, but nice. Anton hugged Aunt

Bridget but Julian was too frightened to go to her and stayed close to Mother.

Before long, the grown-ups and the older children sat down at the table. Anna sidled up to one of her cousins who looked about the same age as she was.

"My name is Anna. What's yours?" she asked.

"Paul."

"Did you like our new church? Isn't it big?"

"Not as big as the one we had in Lipusz, in Poland. That one was twice as big!"

"Do you like your new house?"

"It's all right. But our place in Poland had *two* stories and an attic."

Anna wasn't at all upset at her cousin's words. She had always suspected that things were grand and big and fine in Poland. Father usually sounded sad when he talked about growing up there, but Mother's eyes sparkled when she spoke of her earlier home.

"Tell me all about Poland," pleaded Anna. "Did you live on the big lake, like Father?"

"He was gone before I was born," answered Paul, "but I think he used to live in the same place we did. It was on the part sticking out into the lake, like an island."

"Was the lake bigger than the Mississippi River?" asked Anna. She had only been to the edge of the Mississippi once, last year, but she remembered how endless and wide it had seemed.

"Not quite that big," answered Paul. "The Mississippi is pretty wide. But it's not as big and wide as the Atlantic Ocean. That took us five weeks to cross in the ship!"

"I wish I could cross the ocean in a ship and go to Poland," thought Anna, but she didn't say it aloud.

29

Instead, she continued to question Paul about the long journey, what it was like to live in Poland, and what he used to do there.

Finally, it was their turn to sit down and eat. Mrs. Cierzan heaped their plates with sliced smoked ham, sauerkraut with pearled barley and boiled potatoes. Afterwards, she gave them thick, square chunks of poppy seed cake. Just as they were finishing up the last crumbs, the sound of sleigh bells echoed from the front yard. Mr. Olszewski opened the door and in stepped Mr. Tushner, carrying a huge stone crock in his arms.

"We had some extra sauerkraut and we thought you could put it to good use," he said as he set the crock down in a corner.

"Thanks, neighbor," replied Mr. Olszewski, shaking Mr. Tushner's hand. "Sit down awhile and have something to eat and drink."

"First we have to make some room," said Mother. She turned to the children. "Put on your warm things and go out to play in the snow."

They bundled up again and went out into the yard. Hardly had they started a game of snow tag when another bobsled pulled up in the yard, and then another. In the first one were Mr. Cierzan and the Cierzan children, and in the second the Glenzinski family.

Mr. Cierzan lifted a heavy sack from the sled box.

"Go and ask your father where he wants me to put this," he said to Johnny Olszewski. "It's just a bit of seed grain I thought he could use."

Behind the Glenzinskis' sled was tied a sturdy, stout mare. Mr. Glenzinski undid the rope that went from her bridle to the back sled boards and handed it to Mr. Olszewski as he came out the door.

"Here. You can have her foal if you feed her and bed her down until early summer. I noticed you don't have but one horse, and you'll never get your plowing and planting done without a team."

Mr. Olszewski was speechless with surprise at first. Then he broke into a grin.

"I can't think why I stayed in Canada so long," he said. "You folks around here are the most generous I ever did see."

Other neighbors came in the afternoon, and each brought something to help the new family get a good start. Some carried packets of vegetable seeds, or a bag of potatoes. Others brought the promise of a load of hay or straw.

The grown-ups stayed in the house, but the children went outdoors as soon as they had had a bite to eat. All afternoon they played, chasing each other in the snow, making snow statues, or building forts of packed snow and then defending or attacking the forts with hundreds of snowballs. Whenever they got cold, they ran into the house for a few minutes and Mother or Mrs. Cierzan gave them a cup of warm milk and a slice of bread.

"Winter weddings are even more fun than summer ones," thought Anna.

At dusk, Jacob and Franciszek left to do the chores, and Mary went to milk the cows. Mother wanted to send all the children home, but Anna pleaded with her: "Can't we stay for the dancing? We'll keep out of the way."

"All right, but not too late. I don't want you falling asleep here."

They took turns eating a quick supper of fried potatoes and bacon and then it was time to clear the room. They shoved the table and benches up against the wall and then stacked the chairs in the back bedroom. Mother and Aunt Bridget rolled up the rag rugs and set them under the table.

"That's a good place to sit," said Anna to Julia Cierzan. They crawled under the table and sat on the rolled-up rugs as though they were cushions.

"I want to sit there, too," said Susan Olszewski, so they moved over and let her have some of the space.

Mr. Brom was fingering the keys on his accordion and moving the two endpieces back and forth. The middle was pleated just like the bottom of Mother's best dress. The pleats stretched open and then closed, each time Mr. Brom pulled or pushed on the wooden ends. At last he felt he had the tune right.

"Now for the wedding waltz," he called out, and all the men and women lined up in couples. When the music started, they began to twirl and turn, around and around, circling the room but also making small circles as they wove in and out.

"How is it that they never bump into each other?" wondered Anna. She watched her parents' feet as they danced past. Mother's narrow, neat shoes made two tiny steps and then a long slide. Time and again Father's thick leather boots seemed about to step on Mother's toes, but they never did. They glided along, making the same steps and slides.

"Yoo, hoo, hoo!" yodeled one of the dancers as he made a fine turn.

The music rolled merrily out of the accordion, almost pushing Anna up from her seat.

"Why, it *makes* me want to go in circles," she thought. It was the first time she realized that music could force her body to move. Clasping her arm around Julia, she swayed first to the right and then to the left, tapping her feet in time to the rhythm.

Suddenly, her cousin Paul, who had been standing at the side of the table, dropped down on all fours and peered under the table at the girls.

"I'm tired of standing," he complained. "I want to sit on that rug, too."

The three girls squeezed together and made room for him. At that moment, Aunt Bridget and Mr. Olszewski went waltzing by. Paul squirmed around and would not look at his mother and new stepfather.

"They dance well together," said Anna, not knowing what else to say.

"She danced better in Poland, with Father," muttered Paul.

"Oh, you!" interrupted Susan. "Always bragging about how everything was better in Poland." She sniffed and then got up, edging her way to the bedroom.

Anna felt sorry for Paul. He did seem to brag a lot, but she thought that was only because he missed Poland.

"I'm glad that you're my cousin and that you came from Poland," she whispered. "You can tell me all you want about it, and I won't even get mad if you brag."

So while they watched the dancers whirling and twirling, Anna whispered questions and Paul told her all about the lakes and castles and windmills and ships and grand ladies and gentlemen. The more she heard, the more Anna became convinced: "I just have to go to Poland someday."

The Sound of Seeds

For the rest of the winter and all through early spring, Anna did not see much of their new neighbors, except when they met at church on Sunday. Even then, Father always wanted to hurry home because he was busy preparing for spring planting; they stayed only long enough to exchange a brief hello.

Every spare moment they had, they sorted seeds, so that only the best ones would be planted.

"I don't want to waste my land on poor grain," said Father.

Mother brought out all the flat pans she could find and into each one Father poured a small amount of grain.

"Spread it out carefully and take out the poor

kernels," he instructed. "We want only the longer, plumper ones." With his left hand he shook the pan from side to side while his right hand plucked a half-dozen kernels out of the pan. "See these small, thin, shriveled seeds? We'll throw those in a pail here, to feed to the animals."

They picked in pairs: Franciszek and Pauline, Mary and Barney, and Jacob and Anna. Anton and Julian were still too little to recognize the difference between good and bad seeds.

At first Anna enjoyed picking out the bad kernels. It was like a game. But as March drew to a close, she grew tired of the task.

"Are we almost finished?" she asked Father one day.

"With the wheat, yes. But after that we have to do the barley and the buckwheat and the oats. They must all be ready before Rogation Day, so they can be blessed. And that's only three weeks away now."

During the evenings of Lent, they had sung songs while picking over the seeds. Anna quickly learned the words and melodies. They were usually sad and slow, but she liked them anyway, and she would move her fingers through the seeds at the same steady rhythm as the song.

Easter came and went and Rogation Day was only a few days off. They still had two sacks of buckwheat seeds to cull out. It was much harder to pick out the bad kernels from buckwheat seeds, because they were shaped like tiny, three-sided triangles and they were dark brown. Nor did they roll easily from side to side, like the wheat kernels. Father would toss and shake the pans gently in many directions before he was satisfied that only good seeds remained.

"Here, this pan is picked over," said Jacob, handing

it to his father. Anna looked up expectantly, to see if Father would agree that they had pulled out all the poor kernels.

Instead of shaking the pan, Father reached in and grabbed a small handful of buckwheat seeds.

"These are really fine seeds, don't you think so, Jacob?" asked Father. And with that he tossed the handful into his mouth and began to chew on them.

Anna gasped. "Why are you eating them, Father? These are for growing in the field." Usually she knew better than to question her father, but this time she couldn't stop herself.

Father looked at her seriously. Then he glanced sideways at Jacob and smiled a little. "Buckwheat will grow just about anywhere, so I expect it will do as well inside me as it will in our fields," he said. "I have a pretty good head of hair but it wouldn't hurt to thicken it a bit, would it, Jacob?"

"That might not be a bad idea," answered Jacob. Then he picked up a pinchful of buckwheat seeds, popped them into his mouth and swallowed them. "I always thought it would be fine if I could carry my own shade tree around, so I wouldn't get so hot working out in the fields. Maybe if I let this buckwheat grow tall enough, it'll come out of my ears—a nice, thick clump on each side. That should give a bit of steady shade. What do you say, Franciszek?"

Everyone had stopped picking out seeds. Anna looked from one face to the next: Franciszek, Pauline, Mary, Barney, Jacob and Father. They all stared back at her solemnly. Then Franciszek coughed and stood up quickly.

"I'd better get you some water, Jake, so you can give

those seeds a good start. I'll bring enough for you, too, Father." He stumbled away to the door leading outside, where they kept the water can.

Anna still could not speak. What Father and Jacob had said surely couldn't be true! Buckwheat seeds would not sprout and grow inside of a person, would they? And yet, seeds did grow very quickly, once you put them in the earth and watered them. It was dark and secret deep in the ground, just like it was inside of herself. Sometimes she thought about what was under her skin. Everyone else could see the outside of her but not even she herself could see what was inside. Yet she could feel it.

"I wonder if I could feel something growing inside of me," thought Anna. She looked around for her mother, to ask her, because Mother never teased and always gave an answer to such things. But Mother was in the back bedroom, getting Julian ready for bed.

Franciszek returned with a tin cup full of water.

"Here," he said, handing it to Jacob. "Give those seeds a good watering." Then he burst out laughing. Pauline and Mary and Barney joined in.

"I knew you were only fooling," said Anna. "Seeds can't grow inside of a person."

"Maybe not," said Jacob, "but then I'd like to know what's making all that noise in my belly. Listen!"

Anna stood close to Jacob and waited until everyone was quiet. Gurgle, growl, gurgle! The noises sounded deep and hollow and came right from his middle.

"You hear that? That's just what it sounds like when you bend down low and listen to the seeds growing."

"Now I *know* you are fibbing," laughed Anna. "I've never heard seeds making noises when they grow."

"Did you ever put your head down to the ground and

listen real hard? You can hear them," Jacob assured her.

"Well, hear them or not, we won't get any of these seeds growing unless you finish culling them out," interrupted Father.

That put a stop to their laughing and joking for the moment. When Father spoke like that, he meant business. A little fun was all right, but only if it didn't interfere

too much with their work. Quickly, they went back to their seed pans.

"They were teasing me, I know they were," said Anna to herself. Jacob often tried to fool her into believing something. Still, every now and then, the funny things he told her did come true. Last year, he had laughed and said: "Just wait! Pretty soon an Indian woman will bring you a new baby brother or sister!" For two days he had said that but she hadn't believed him at all. And then on the third morning she had awakened and she did have a new baby brother.

"But I didn't see any Indian woman," she had insisted.

"Well, where do you suppose baby Julian got that pretty Indian blanket, then?" Jacob had asked. So she supposed he might be right.

"Could it be the same now with the seeds?" Anna wondered silently as she carefully picked away at the last of the buckwheat kernels.

A few days later Father and Jacob were busy planting. The wheat and oats went on their best fields, where all the stumps were cleared out, starting right in back of the barn and stretching out almost as far as Olszewski's land. The corn and buckwheat they planted on the smaller fields on the hillsides, where there were still occasional tree stumps that would have to be grubbed out some day. The clover seeds were very tiny so they hadn't had to pick them over. Father sowed the clover in the lower meadow.

In the garden Mother planted some of her vegetable seeds: peas, radishes, lettuce, onions, beans, carrots, beets and rutabagas. Later she would set out the tiny cucumber and cabbage plants that were already sprouting in a box by the kitchen window.

"Will the seeds start growing right away?" asked Anna.

"As soon as they are warmed by the sun," answered Mother. "That's why I plant them with just a thin layer of soil on top. You'll see them come up in a few days."

For the next few mornings Anna checked the garden very carefully. She always looked to make sure no one was watching her and then she leaned her ear over the spots where she had seen Mother sprinkle the seeds.

"I still don't hear anything," she mumbled.

On the fourth morning she saw wispy rows of feathery green leaves no bigger than the tip of her little finger. In the bean row there were tiny curled rings of yellow-green. She knelt down and leaned over the bean plants, trying not to move. Faintly, as though it were coming from inside a box, she heard the sound of gentle popping: Pock! Pock! Pock!

Hardly believing what she heard, she moved farther down the bean row and once more put her ear close to the ground. There it was again—the same soft sound: Pock! Pock! Pock!

"Jacob was right!" she whispered softly. "I *can* hear the seeds growing."

She continued kneeling there, listening to the muffled popping and the other whispery sounds made by the tiny leaves as they rubbed against the earth. All the other sounds of the farm faded into the distance. She felt as though she were the only person in the world and all these seeds were growing just for her.

"What are you doing there?" Mother's sharp, questioning voice startled her so that she tumbled over onto her side.

41

"I was listening to the seeds," admitted Anna.

"Listening to the seeds?" Mother looked puzzled.

"Jacob said you could hear them growing, and you can, if you put your ear up close." Anna's voice was filled with wonder.

"Yes, I suppose you can," answered Mother with a smile. She stood there quietly, surveying her garden with pride.

"Can seeds grow inside a person?" asked Anna suddenly. She had to be sure.

"What do you mean?" For some reason, Mother's voice sounded flustered and nervous.

"Well, if I swallowed a seed of something, would it grow inside me?"

"So that's what you've been worrying about!" Mother laughed gently. "No, Anna. If you swallow seeds they go through you just like the rest of your food. We all eat seeds sometimes. Poppy seed cake is full of them."

Anna breathed a sigh of relief. Of course! Why hadn't she thought of that when Father and Jacob were teasing her?

For a few more minutes, Anna and her mother stood there silently, surrounded by the soft sounds and the pale colors of the growing young plants. She thought about the mysterious power that made seeds grow. And the more she thought, the more she began to realize that Father and Jacob had been trying to tell her about that wonderful power of seeds.

"That must be why they tease me," she thought in surprise. "When it's hard to think of the right words to explain something, they try to tell me by teasing." She made up her mind not to let it bother her so much any more.

Herding Sheep

"Do you think she should go?" asked Mother.

"She has to learn some time," replied Father. "I won't be able to spare Barney when harvest time comes."

Anna was silent while her parents discussed whether she should help Barney take the sheep and lambs to the pasture every day until she learned how to do it by herself. She wouldn't have to stay with the sheep all day, any more than Barney did. Johnny Olszewski did that. But someone had to guide them each morning to the pasture, where they could join the rest of the flock, and then bring them back in the evening.

"Well, I guess it won't hurt," agreed Mother reluctantly.

The next morning, after breakfast, Pauline let out the three cows and two calves and prodded them down toward the small sloping pasture below the house, right next to the creek. Later in the summer she would have to take them to pasture farther away, but for now they could stay nearby.

Barney and Anna, meanwhile, took their short sticks and guided the sheep along the path leading toward the Olszewskis' farm. There were three ewes with their lambs and two yearling sheep.

"Watch them closely," warned Barney. "You'll soon see that sheep are a lot harder to manage than cows."

They trudged along the narrow path. On one side of them was the long field of wheat, spread out like an endless brown carpet with speckles and patches of grass. On the other side were the fields of corn and buckwheat, and behind them the woods.

The yearling lambs wanted to wander off into the fields to nibble on the plants growing there. First they would run to the left and try the wheat. Then, as soon as Anna chased them back onto the path, they would stray to the corn plants on the right. Back and forth they scampered, and back and forth Anna raced, trying to keep them away from Father's crops. Barney stayed mostly behind them, keeping them in line with his stick.

"Watch out! They're off into the wheat again," called Barney as Anna lagged behind for a moment.

"You run after them. I'm tired!" complained Anna.

"Father says you have to learn how to do it."

"But you're supposed to help."

"Then you won't know how to do it on your own," Barney insisted, and he made her do all the running.

When they were halfway to the pasture, Anna saw a

boy prodding some sheep up the hill on the small path between the corn and buckwheat. It was Paul Jaszewski, bringing his family's sheep to join the flock. He did not see Barney coming along behind.

"Say, aren't you kind of small to be bringing the sheep out?" Paul called to Anna.

Anna didn't know what to answer. She wanted to be considered grown-up enough to be able to do it. On the other hand, she could see it was not the easiest job in the world. Those pesky lambs just would not stay in line.

"She's not alone," called Barney as he came up. "I'm teaching her how to do it."

"Shall we wait for John?" asked Paul. "I saw him coming up not too far behind me."

"John who?" asked Anna.

"John Dorawa."

"He brings his sheep way over here?" Anna was surprised.

"He does have a long way to walk," agreed Paul.

They let the sheep graze for a few minutes on the grassy mounds lining the path. Now that there were more of them, they seemed to stay together better. Every so often, though, one of the sheep would stray closer and closer to the wheat plants, and Anna had to run and prod it back toward the flock.

She peered down the hill and saw John slowly guiding his eight sheep and lambs toward the larger flock.

"Hurry up!" she called. But sheep cannot be hurried if they don't want to be. It seemed a very long time before John had them all safely up the hill and joined with the rest of the flock. Now there were more than twenty sheep and lambs moving slowly along the path.

"Hey, since there are three of you, I think I'll let you

take them from here," said Paul. "I want to get back to help Father."

"All by ourselves?" questioned Anna in surprise. Paul was the biggest and oldest and strongest. Would they be able to manage all those sheep without him?

"Sure, go ahead," agreed Barney and John. "We'll take over." Anna didn't know it but the boys often took turns herding the flock for the last stretch, before they came to the pasture.

"So long, then," said Paul, and he turned back toward the Jaszewski farm.

Barney, Anna and John continued on their way.

"Of course, if the wolves come, you know what to do, don't you?" asked Barney.

"Wolves?" cried Anna.

"He's just fooling," John assured her. "I've never seen any wolves around here." But Anna could see that he looked a little scared himself.

They swung around behind the wheat field and over to the left, toward the back part of Cierzan's farm. Anna remembered this path because it went straight along the edge of the Olszewskis' land.

Suddenly the sheep were no longer docile. Two baby lambs went frolicking and tumbling into a small ravine and Anna circled around to turn them back. At the same time, one of the yearling lambs leaped and ran into the Olszewskis' oats field and John hurried after it, trying to get to it before it could chomp on the oats. One of the baby lambs scampered after him. Though he tried to chase it back, the lamb kept right on following him, like a pet.

Every few steps they took after that, it seemed that one or two lambs, and sometimes even one of the older sheep, would try to run off in the wrong direction. Barney, Anna and John were exhausted from all the chasing they had to do.

"What's gotten into those sheep?" asked Barney. "They never acted up like this before."

"They're just feeling good, I guess," answered John.

Anna agreed with him. Sometimes on bright, early summer days like this one, she, too, felt like running and hopping and skipping about for no reason.

Finally they reached the pasture where Johnny Olszewski waited with the Cierzans' sheep. His father didn't have any sheep yet, so Johnny was working to earn some. After he took care of the flock all summer, each farmer would give him one lamb.

As they reached the pasture, instead of joining up together, the lambs from the two flocks started butting and chasing each other in all directions.

"I told Father he has to get me a dog," said Johnny disgustedly. "I'll never keep this many lambs out of mischief all by myself."

"We'll help you get them together and move them down to that corner by the spring. They should stay put there quite a while. There's plenty to graze on." Barney offered the suggestion and immediately moved to the far right to round up a half-dozen lambs.

Anna and John Dorawa swung far around to the left and started to prod the sheep that had strayed there. John's pet lamb ran at his side, like a puppy. Johnny Olszewski stayed behind the flock, guiding them forward slowly and preventing them from going back in the direction they came from.

"Go on, go on!" Anna prodded a small lamb with her stick. It would not budge.

"Get moving, I say!" She smacked it on the rump.

Around whirled the lamb, putting its head down and making as if to butt her. Anna was so startled she dropped her stick and moved back.

"Are you scared of such a little thing?" John chided her. "He can't butt hard. You'd sooner knock him over than he would be able to do anything to you."

48

Back and forth they chased, moving the lambs closer and closer to the spring that emptied out into a bubbling little creek.

"I've got to have a drink," called John. He was closest to the spring and could hear the cool splashing and gurgling of the water as it fell on the stones. He went to the edge of the bank out of which the water tumbled, and leaned far over, letting the water splash over his head and face, as well as into his mouth.

"Aaahh! That feels and tastes good," he called out as he came up for air. "Come on and try it." Once again he bent down to get another drink.

Anna jogged toward the spring, but so did the frisky lamb that had been following John all morning. Head down, it ran straight for John. Before Anna could call out a warning, the lamb butted John from behind. Over he went, somersaulting into the creek a few feet below. The lamb stood there, looking down at him.

"Maaaa!" it bleated, in such a funny way that it seemed to be laughing at him.

Anna burst into giggles as she came up to the edge of the bank. She could see that John was not hurt. He sat there, glaring up at the lamb while the sparkling water flowed and bubbled all around him, wetting his pants and shoes.

"I thought you said the lambs can't butt hard," said Anna.

John didn't answer her. Instead, he glared up at both Anna and the lamb. Then he stood up and jumped out of the creek. The mud had left deep black stains up and down the back of his pants. He tried to rub them away, but rubbing only made the stains worse. Finally, he gave up and scrambled up the bank.

They herded the last lambs into the pasture corner and left them with Johnny Olszewski. Barney and Anna did not say much to John as they walked back home. They could see he was upset and mad.

Anna tried hard not to giggle. "Why is it?" she wondered, "that if you take a tumble yourself you don't think it's funny, but when someone else does, you always have to laugh?"

They separated at the path crossing where they had met John earlier. As soon as John had gone a distance, Barney and Anna looked at each other and burst out laughing.

"I hope he doesn't get a licking," said Anna, feeling guilty about the laughter.

"He'll live through it," was all Barney said.

100th Birthday

"Have you packed the tin cups?" asked Mother as she carefully sliced a long chunk of dried beef.

"Yes," answered Pauline. "They're in the basket."

"And what about the linen cloth, Anna? Did you find it in the chest?"

"Yes, Mother. It's in the basket, too. At the bottom." Anna sighed. It seemed to take forever for the whole family to get ready. She was sure they would be late for the Fourth of July celebration in Dodge.

Mother placed the slices of dried beef in a small crock, sprinkling each layer with vinegar. The crock was almost full, but still she kept on slicing.

In the back bedroom, Father was changing into his

good suit. In the kitchen, Mary was tying chunks of bread into a clean white dishcloth. Outside, Jacob and Franciszek were hitching up Lord and Lady to the wagon, and decorating it with leaves and branches. Anton and Julian were so excited by all the preparations, they kept running back and forth, into the house and then out again.

At last everything was packed and put into the wagon. It looked very festive with its tall sprays of green leaves sticking up from each corner. They climbed up to their places and when they were all settled, Father turned the horses and down the road they went.

Anna had never been to a Fourth of July celebration, so she didn't know what to expect. She was excited because she was going to see something new. She stared at Jacob, sitting at the end of the wagon, looking backward, his long legs hanging down. The tree branches that were fastened at each side of the wagon met over his head. When he turned around, Anna and Barney, sitting in front of him on the wagon bed, thought he looked like a deer in the forest, peering through a cover of brushy leaves.

Ahead of them on the road was another wagon. It, too, had thick, leafy branches stuck into the back corners. The closer they came to Dodge, the more wagons Anna could see, behind them and ahead of them.

"Is *everybody* coming to town?" she asked.

"Sure. Nobody wants to miss the parade," said Jacob.

"What's a parade?"

"You'll soon see."

At the edge of the town of Dodge, Father stopped the horses behind another wagon. The wagons behind them pulled up and stopped, too. Now they were waiting in the middle of a long, curving line of wagons and buggies, each decorated with greenery. Anna stood up and stretched her neck as far to the left as she could. She saw that the first buggy was decorated with special care.

"Look! The flags!"

Everyone strained and stretched to watch as several men fastened two flags on poles to the sides of the first buggy. They fluttered and waved in the gentle breeze.

"We got here just in time," said Father. "We won't have to wait long now."

Ten minutes later, they heard a muffled bang. It came from the center of town, and sounded like a gun. Slowly, the wagons and buggies started to move forward.

As soon as their wagon got close to Dodge, Anna gasped with pleasure. In front of all the houses, on both sides of the road, someone had propped up huge evergreen branches, as tall as trees. They arched over the narrow road, so that the tips met high overhead. When the wagon passed underneath, it was like entering a secret forest.

In front of each house people were standing and waving. Some of them waved flags of red, white and blue. Whenever a wagon passed with someone in it that they recognized, the children called out or cheered.

Under the canopy of green the wagons were driven. Then they were turned right to cross the railroad tracks. Here there were no special trees or decorative branches because the drivers had to be able to see if a train was coming. But once past the tracks, they saw that the depot on the left and the stores and houses on the right were hidden by more branches of evergreens, tall silvery poplars, or the lacy fronds of willows.

Again they entered what seemed like a green tunnel,

speckled with sunlight sifting through the quivering leaves. Suddenly, Father swerved to the right. Coming toward them from the opposite direction was another line of wagons, led by a buggy with two flags.

"Did they turn around?" asked Anna, puzzled.

"No, that's the other part of the parade, coming from the other side of town. The gun was the signal for both to start," explained Jacob.

The two parades passed each other and the passengers called out or cheered as soon as they saw someone they knew. Standing in the back of the wagon, Anna was so excited she had to grab hold of Jacob, for fear of tumbling over.

On to the end of the street they went, under the bower of green. Then, across the tracks at the far end of Dodge and back down the other street, behind the depot. And all the time the second parade was doing the same thing, only in the opposite direction. Three times the wagons went around, with people cheering and laughing and calling out to each other. In and out of the green tunnels they wove, enjoying the cool, secret feeling they got each time they entered one. Anna wished they could go around a few more times but Father said the horses needed to rest.

He stopped the wagon in front of the school and everyone got out. After lining the wagon up between two buggies, Father and Jacob unhitched the horses and unbuckled the harness, leaving only the bridles on their necks.

"Take them over to Bambenek's field and tether them. He offered to let all the horses graze there today."

Behind the school was a small field where everyone was gathering. Each family spread out an old blanket or cloth and placed their food in the center. Then they stood around, looking expectantly at the rest of the crowd. Anna did not know why they were waiting. She was hungry and wanted to start eating. Just as she was about to ask one of her sisters why they had to wait, a tall, sturdy man came walking up to Father.

"Hello there, Frank Pellowski! I haven't seen you in a long time."

"Well, Albert Bautsch, as I live and breathe! What are you doing here?" Father stretched out his hand.

"We got to thinking about how we first came out this way, back in '62, and we decided we should come and celebrate the Fourth with you folks." Mr. Bautsch shook Father's hand as he answered.

Anna stared at him. He was speaking in Polish, but it sounded so strange, she could hardly understand him.

"Why is he talking like that?" whispered Anna to her mother, as Mr. Bautsch continued chatting with Father.

"Because he comes from Silesia," said Mother. "That's a different part of Poland than where we come from. We are from Pomerania."

"I didn't know there were different parts of Poland," said Anna. She still hoped to go there someday, but she had thought everyone in Poland would speak the same way she did.

Father and Mr. Bautsch soon had to stop talking because a man stood up on a wagon pulled up at the side of the school. It was Mr. Baumgartner, the town clerk.

"Ladies and Gentlemen!" he called out, first in German and then in Polish, Bohemian and Norwegian. Finally he said it in English. He began to mix up words in all five languages. Anna could only understand Polish, but somehow she could make out what Mr. Baumgartner was saying, even when he used German and Bohemian and English words. He talked about freedom and about liberty and about independence. It sounded a little like Father Snigourski when he preached a sermon in church. He ended with a cheer: "Happy one-hundred-year birthday to America!" Everyone clapped and cheered with him.

"America is having a birthday?" asked Anna in

surprise. She had never heard of a country having a birthday.

"Yes, today it is one hundred years old," replied Father. "That's what the Fourth of July is—the birthday of America."

"And now it's time to have a birthday feast," said Mother. She turned to Mr. Bautsch. "Won't you join us?"

"Thank you kindly, but my family is settled down over there," he answered, pointing to a group seated on a blanket under a tree. "I had better hurry or the eats will be all gone before I get a taste." With a wave of his hand he moved off.

Mother spread out the linen cloth and on it she placed the food.

"Help yourselves!" she said. They could eat everything with their fingers: tasty, crunchy pieces of fried chicken; chewy, tangy slices of dried beef; thick chunks of bread spread with butter; sugary squares of *pączki* that were puffy and light. From the well at the side of the school Jacob pumped up drinking water, so cold that it almost hurt Anna's teeth as she drank it from a tin cup.

BOOM! As they were finishing their picnic dinner a tremendous blast sounded through the town. It was much louder than the gunshot that had started the parade.

"Good heavens! What was that?" exclaimed Mother.

"Charlie Kassimor is probably firing the anvils," explained Father.

"I heard he wants to do it at least ten times," said Jacob.

"He'd have to find a lot of foolish men to help him, then, and I'm not one of them. That's dangerous, firing with gunpowder like that. I'd rather have a good game of cards." Father looked around to see if he could find some neighbors or friends willing to play euchre with him.

"I think I'll go have a look," said Jacob, and he sauntered off. Franciszek and Barney tagged along behind him.

Anna was just wondering if she could ask Mother for permission to go when Mary and Pauline got up.

"Let's take a walk over there."

"Is that all right, Mother?"

Mother smiled and nodded her head. "Julian and Anton will probably have a nap. I can manage."

"No nap!" insisted Anton. "I want to see the boom!"

"Come along, then," laughed Pauline and Anna as they each took hold of one of his hands and set off for the blacksmith shop. They did not have far to walk. Down the road, past the general store, was Mr. Kassimor's shop.

Usually the iron anvils stood inside, next to the hot fire. Today, they rested on a big block of wood in front of the shop. One of the anvils was upside down. Anna watched with her brothers and sisters as Mr. Kassimor sprinkled gunpowder in the hole on the bottom of the anvil. Then he put a metal ring over the hole and sprinkled a trail of gunpowder out to the edge of the anvil.

"Here, give me a hand with this, someone," begged Mr. Kassimor as he turned to the second anvil. Jacob stepped forward and grabbed hold of one end. Sweating and straining, they lifted it up and placed it right on top of the upside-down anvil. Their muscles bulged with the effort. The anvil wasn't very big, but it was quite heavy.

As soon as it was in place, Mr. Kassimor went into his shop and picked up a long poker that was sticking out from the open fire. The end that had been in the hot coals was red and shimmery.

"Stand back, everyone, and cover your ears if you don't want them blown out," warned Mr. Kassimor.

Quickly they all stepped far back into the road and held their hands over their ears.

Sssss! went the hot poker as it touched the trail of gunpowder spilling out over the side of the anvil. Mr. Kassimor hopped back out of the way.

BOOM! The top anvil was lifted six feet into the air as an explosion echoed and re-echoed through the town. Even standing fifty feet away, Anna could feel the force of the blast press against her like a strong, quick wind. Her ears tingled and after she took her hands away and waited for a few moments, they were still ringing with the sound of the big BOOM!

Once more the men moved in close to the anvils and prepared for another firing. Then Mrs. Kassimor stepped out of the house at the side of the blacksmith shop.

"Charles, enough is enough!" she scolded him laughingly.

"This will be the last one," promised Mr. Kassimor. "Anyway, that's the last of the gunpowder I have on hand."

Carefully the men sprinkled the gunpowder in the hole and along the side and then replaced the second anvil on top.

"I'll get the poker," said Jacob, and he hurried to take it out of the fire. "May I light this one?" he asked Mr. Kassimor.

"All right, but be careful. Jump back as soon as you touch the gunpowder," cautioned Mr. Kassimor. He waved everyone back out into the road and they waited silently as Jacob positioned the poker.

Sssss! Again there was a sizzling sound as the gunpowder took fire. Only this time it formed a small ball of fiery sparks that bounced off the anvil. Jacob jumped back, but not quite fast enough.

BOOM! The explosion came at the same moment that the glowing, fiery sparks landed on Jacob's arm. Everyone gasped and stood rooted like trees. Everyone except Jacob, that is. He ran to the tank of water and plunged his arm deep into it.

"Did you get hurt?" asked Mr. Kassimor as he came to his senses and hurried over to Jacob.

"No, just singed a little," said Jacob, laughing in a shaky, scared way.

Everyone clustered around him to look at his right arm. The hairs were singed right down to his skin.

"Good thing there was less gunpowder for this last shot," said Mr. Kassimor, before he turned to the crowd. "That's it for this Fourth of July, folks. All's well that ends well."

Slowly the throng around the blacksmith shop began to break up. Pauline and Mary took Anton by the hand and turned to go back to Mother. Anna followed them silently. Her ears were still ringing and she felt as though everything around her were far away.

"I wonder if they have Fourth of July in Poland?" she thought. She would have to ask Mother sometime.

Wolves and Hail

After the excitement of the Fourth of July, summer seemed calm, until it was time for the harvest. First to ripen was the wheat, and for several days everyone worked in the fields, gathering up the bundles and putting them in shocks. Mother and Mary and Pauline helped, too, so Anna and Barney took turns watching Julian and Anton.

Anna didn't like being out in the wheat field now that the stalks were all cut down. The stubble left on the field hurt her bare feet when she tried to walk on it. She preferred to stay at the edge, under the shade of one of the trees.

No sooner was the wheat all neatly shocked than Father said it was time to start on the oats.

"And the barley will be ready in a day or so, too. We'll have to hop to get it all done in time. Cierzan told me the threshing rig is coming to the valley next week."

Every day they worked steadily from sunup to sundown. Mother stopped long enough to make dinner and supper. Mary and Pauline left the field at four o'clock to feed the pigs and chickens and to feed and milk the cows. Anna left with them, but walked in the opposite direction. She was going all by herself now to get the sheep each evening.

The next week, Father and Jacob were gone for the first three days. On Monday they threshed at Tushner's; on Tuesday they moved to the Wickas' farm; on Wednesday the machine was pulled to Cierzan's front yard. Anna could see it through the trees, and could hear the loud, rackety noises it made as it separated the grain from the straw. But she did not have time to go over and look at it close up. She was too busy helping Mother with all the baking and cooking that had to be done for the next day.

In the evening the men moved the machine up to their farm. It took six horses to get it up the hill and into the yard next to the barn.

The following morning, before the men started threshing, Anna rounded up the sheep and guided them to the path along the wheat field. She knew now which lambs to watch carefully, and always caught them and prodded them back into line before they wandered too far away. Where the paths crisscrossed, she met Johnny Olszewski and together they steered the sheep to the pasture at the back of Jaszewski's farm. John Dorawa was just leaving as they arrived.

"Got to hurry," he called. "We're threshing with you today."

Anna hurried home, too. By the time she got back, the men were busy stuffing the bundles into the machine, and catching the grain in sacks as it came out the chute. Straw was blowing out of the other side and a thick, chaffy dust filled the air. Even though the noise hurt her ears and she could hardly breathe in the thick air, she couldn't stop herself from watching the movement of the men and the horses and the machine.

"Don't stand there gawping! Come and help us," called Pauline.

"I'm coming," answered Anna. She was really glad to get away from the noise and the choking dust.

She helped Pauline line up some long planks on sawhorses. That would be the table where the men would eat.

"Now help me make the benches," said Pauline.

They went to the woodpile, selected three sturdy chunks of wood, and rolled them one by one next to the plank table. After they were properly spaced, one at each end and one in the middle, they put a plank over all three.

"This should do fine," said Pauline, as she sat down on the makeshift bench.

Bump! Thump! The plank flew off and Pauline landed on her bottom, sitting in the dirt. Anna wanted to ask if she was hurt, but all she could do was laugh.

"Just laugh! I'll make you try it next," said Pauline as she got up and dusted herself off. She looked closely at the chunks of wood and then took out one from the end.

"This is the culprit. It's too short."

They rolled it back and selected another that worked much better. Then they made a similar bench for the other side of the table.

"You sit on it this time," suggested Pauline.

Anna first checked to see that the plank rested on all three chunks of wood. Then she sat down daintily at one end, where the plank extended a bit over the stump.

Whee! Up flew the plank at the other end, like a seesaw, and down she tumbled.

"You did that on purpose," accused Anna.

"No, I didn't."

"Yes, you did."

"I didn't."

"Girls, stop your quarreling and get busy making the second table. One won't be enough for all those men," Mother's voice called sternly from the front door.

They made a second plank table and benches and this time all worked well. At noon, the men stopped working and washed their hands and faces in a small basin.

"Ah, that feels good," they said as Anna brought a fresh pitcher of cool water for each one.

They took seats on both sides of the plank tables and began to eat from the big platters and pots of food that Mother and Mary and Pauline brought out. At first, no one spoke. They were all too busy eating. Anna scurried back and forth, filling and refilling the two pitchers, one with milk and the other with cool spring water.

"Did I see right this morning, Frank?" asked one of the men. "Was this little girl of yours taking the sheep to pasture all by herself?"

"Yes," answered Father proudly. "She can do it all on her own."

"Well, I'm not too sure that's a good idea," said the man. "We were over by Waumandee last week and one farmer told us his sheep were attacked by a pack of wolves—about ten of them. They got away with four sheep."

Anna stood stock-still. Was the man joking? No, he looked very serious.

Father was looking serious, too. "By Waumandee, you say?"

"Yes, no more than ten miles from here as the crow flies."

"Who was herding?"

"Two of his children—a boy and a girl."

"Did they get hurt?"

"No. The wolves didn't go for them. They only attacked the sheep."

Father was silent a moment. Then he looked at the other table, where Franciszek was eating.

"I hate to spare Franciszek, he's so handy in the grain bin. But he'll have to go, I guess. Barney can't handle the gun yet."

Anna looked anxiously at Father. Did that mean she wouldn't have to go? She didn't want to, now that she had heard about the wolves. But Father looked at her and said firmly: "You go along, too, so you can do the chasing. No harm will come to you, as long as you do what Franciszek says."

For the rest of that afternoon, Anna tried not to think about the wolves, but the harder she tried, the more she found herself picturing packs of wolves running after her and the sheep.

"Maybe if I hide when it's time to go, Franciszek will leave without me," she thought. Then she made up her mind to be brave.

"Bah! I don't care about any old wolves!" she said. But inside, she still had a trembly feeling.

At mid-afternoon, Mr. Olszewski brought one wagon load of grain bundles he had to thresh and Mr. Dorawa and John drove up with two loads from their fields.

"We'd have waited until tomorrow, and threshed at Jaszewski's, but I don't like the smell of the wind," said Mr. Dorawa. "I think we're due for a storm."

"You think so?" asked Father, looking questioningly at the northwest.

The other men also stared in that direction. There was not a cloud to be seen in the sky.

"I think it will hold off for a few days yet," said one of them.

By four o'clock, though, there was a thin, dark line of clouds all along the edge of the northwestern sky. Father stared at it long and hard before he went into the house. When he came out he was carrying his gun.

"Here, Frank. Should you see a sign of wolves, fire a shot and take the sheep to the nearest farm, as fast as you can. But don't fire unless you have to. And hurry! I don't like the look of those clouds building up."

Anna could see that Franciszek felt proud and grown-up from the way he took the gun. He liked to be called Frank, like Father.

"Franciszek is a name for babies," he always protested when Mother called him that. Anna always thought of him as Franciszek, too. Somehow, she couldn't call him by any other name, even now, after Father had called him Frank.

The threshing was almost finished, so Mr. Dorawa hitched up his two wagons and prepared to leave. They were piled high with straw and on top of the straw lay the sacks of grain.

"I'll drive one team for you," said Mr. Jaszewski. "Then John can go directly for the sheep."

"Let's go," said Franciszek, and he hurried to the

path behind the barn. Anna and John could hardly keep up with him.

Suddenly the wind picked up. The faster they walked, the harder the wind came blowing at them. At first it blew in their faces, but when they turned east down the path toward Jaszewski's back pasture, it blew in their backs. Now Anna could hardly keep from tumbling over onto her face. She could see that Franciszek had trouble balancing the gun. The wind wanted to tear it out of his hands. It grew darker by the minute. By the time they reached the flock of sheep, the sun was entirely hidden behind thick, deep blue clouds that tumbled and turned and churned like a giant kettle of boiling indigo dye with lumps of wool in it.

The wind grew icy cold, and Anna shivered. Quickly, they separated the flock into two. Anna and Franciszek and Johnny Olszewski took their half and John Dorawa and Paul Jaszewski took the other.

"Anna, go right! Johnny, go left! Keep them close together!" Franciszek yelled, but his voice was half swallowed by the wind.

The frightened sheep did not want to stay in the path, but pushed toward a sheltered place under some trees. Fortunately, they stayed in a flock. Urgently, Anna, Franciszek and Johnny pushed and shoved and poked the sheep to keep them moving in the right direction.

Suddenly a stroke of lightning pierced the black cloud and zinged downward, like a fiery pitchfork flung at the earth. A tremendous crackle and booming followed as thunder surrounded them with its echoes from the hills and ravines. The noise finally made the sheep pick up speed, but still, it seemed to take forever before they reached the crossing paths.

"Come with us!" yelled Franciszek to Johnny.

Johnny shook his head. He was anxious to get the sheep safely back to the Cierzans'.

An icy stinging struck at Anna's face and arms.

"Hail!" she shrieked.

"Come with us!" repeated Franciszek. "You've got to!"

Johnny stubbornly shook his head again. Hurriedly, he separated out the sheep that were to go with him and prodded them off in a westerly direction.

The hail continued to beat down on them, first the size of little peas, then growing as big as beans. It hurt as it pinged into Anna's face. She held up her hands to shield her eyes so she could see.

The sheep did not like the hail either. The three lambs were bleating and trying to hide under their mothers, who huddled close together and no longer tried to move away from the path. But that was the trouble! They did not want to move at all.

"Ow! Ow!" Anna cried out as several large pieces of hail pelted her head. She hadn't meant to cry, but the hail hurt so much she couldn't help it. Peering out from under her shaded eyes she looked at the hail. Now it was the size of cherries.

"It's not wolves we have to worry about," she thought. "No wolves would come out in this weather." The hail continued to beat down on her, lashing every part of her body. Lightning zigzagged through the air and seemed to be all around them. Ahead of her and to the left, in a small ravine separating the fields of corn and oats, Anna saw a tall, leafy tree.

"Let's go stand under that," she shouted to Franciszek.

"No!" he screamed in answer. ". . . worst . . . lightning . . ." He tried to tell her something but his words were blown away by the wind.

Still the hailstones pounded down, harder than ever. One lamb was hit by so many it fell to the ground, stunned. Franciszek tried to pick it up, but it was hard to carry both the lamb and the gun.

69

A second little lamb went down, and Anna hurried to it. She tried to cradle it in her arms, but the lamb was so heavy she could take only a few steps at a time before she had to stop and rest. Step by step they moved forward. At this rate it would take them a long time to reach home. Anna didn't know if she could make it. Her body throbbed from the beating of the hailstones and her arms ached from trying to carry the lamb.

"Hey, I'm coming!" Jacob's voice came faintly from the path ahead of them. Soon he came into view, struggling against the wind, with his arms full of old blankets. Quickly he draped a blanket over Anna, and another over Franciszek, the lamb and the gun. He put a third over his own head and picked up the other two lambs, one in each arm.

"Keep prodding the lead ewe! Run alongside her," shouted Jacob to Anna. "Got to keep them moving!"

She picked up a stick and began to whip the ewe. Though she did not want to hurt it, there was no other way to get the small flock moving faster, so they could get to the safety of the barn. At last the ewe broke into a trot, and Anna trotted alongside. Now the sheep were all moving quickly and soon Anna could see Father up ahead, coming around the barn.

"To the house!" he ordered Anna. He turned to Franciszek and took the lamb from his arms. "You, too!"

Leaning against each other, Anna and Franciszek stumbled toward the house. They were too tired to run. At the door Mother was waiting for them. She breathed a prayer of relief and then hurried to help Anna out of her clothes. Franciszek fell into a chair and the gun clattered to the floor. His hands were trembling so hard he could no longer hold on to it.

Soon they were both sitting next to the stove, bundled in warm quilts and sipping cups of hot milk. They still shivered and shook so much, Pauline and Mary had to hold the cups for them.

By the time Father and Jacob came in, the storm had passed. Hailstones covered the ground but they were melting fast, because the sun was already peeping out at the edge of the clouds as they moved to the east.

"Never saw anything come and go so fast," said Father, shaking his head.

"Are the lambs all right?" asked Anna weakly.

"Yes, they're fine. They started frisking around as soon as they were safe in the barn," Jacob reassured her. Then he turned to Mother. "You should have seen her, trying to carry a lamb that weighs almost as much as she does. She wouldn't give up."

Mother could only cluck her tongue and wipe her eyes.

Father and Jacob stayed in the house a few more minutes, talking about the terrible storm and sharing in the gladness that it was over, with no one hurt and their animals and grain safely tucked away. Then Father moved to the door.

"Well, better get a move on. We have to get the threshing machine to Jaszewski's place before dark. Poor fellow! After all that hail he'll be lucky if there's anything left to thresh."

But that evening they learned something surprising. Mr. Jaszewski had lost hardly any wheat because the cloud of hail had passed behind his fields. Some of the shocks were toppled by the wind, and a few had gotten wet, but most were all right.

"Isn't that the quirkiest thing," said Father after he

returned from moving the threshing machine. "Just a hundred yards away the fields were covered with hail, but his grain was spared. He's a mighty happy man, I can tell you."

Johnny Olszewski had not been so lucky. One of the Cierzans' lambs caught in the hailstorm had died. Anna found out about it the next day, when she and Barney took the sheep out as usual. Mother didn't want her to go, but Anna insisted she felt fine.

"What are you going to do?" she asked Johnny when he told her about the dead lamb.

"Nothing I can do. I'll get one less lamb at the end, that's all." He turned his face away, so Anna and Barney could not see that he was ready to cry.

Anna knew how he must feel. She would have felt terrible if one of their lambs had not survived the ordeal. She wanted to tell him that, but she didn't know how. So she just walked quietly along beside him, thinking how strange it was that their lambs had come through the storm safely, while his had not. She could not understand why the lamb had died. Later, when she asked about it, Mother only said: "The ways of the Lord are mysterious indeed."

Jacob Goes Away

"Do you have to go?" Anna asked Jacob.

He was packing up a satchel of his extra shirts and underwear, while Mother made up a parcel of food.

"I don't have to. I want to," replied Jacob. "I need to earn some money and the lumber camps offer the best wages."

"And the most danger, too," said Mother. She didn't want Jacob to work with the lumbermen.

"Watch carefully," she warned. "And mind your language! Don't you start swearing like some of those men."

Jacob nodded his head in agreement. Anna had never heard hard swearing. She wanted to know what it sounded like, but she didn't want Jacob to speak like that. From what Mother said, it must be terrible.

"And don't forget church on Sunday," continued Mother.

Again Jacob nodded his head. He turned to face everyone lined up in front of the house.

"Well, so long till I see you again," he said, and then turned around and started down the road. Anna followed him.

"I'll walk with you to the curve," she said. She meant the first curve in the valley road.

They walked for a moment in silence.

"Why do you want to earn some money?" she asked.

Jacob laughed. "Because I need it. I won't be living here forever, you know. I want to go off on my own some day."

"Maybe he wants to go to Poland, too," thought Anna, but she was fearful of asking him right out. Instead, she asked him: "Where will you go?"

"Oh, I don't know yet."

"Will you take me with you?"

"Would you like to go somewhere?"

"Yes, to Poland," she blurted out.

"To Poland!" Jacob threw back his head and guffawed. "Well, I hardly think I'm going that far. But if I ever do go, I'll take you with me." Then he laughed harder than ever as though he knew something Anna didn't.

Anna couldn't figure out why he was laughing. Was he teasing?

"Do you promise?" she asked.

"Promise what?"

"That if you ever go to Poland, you'll take me with you."

"It's a promise," said Jacob, but he continued laughing and chuckling. They came to the curve.

"Goodbye, Jacob," called Anna.

Jacob was still shaking with laughter so he turned and waved instead of answering. Then he was gone.

Anna walked slowly back up the road toward the house, wondering what Jacob found so funny. He had been born on the ship, when Mother and Father were coming from Poland to America. Mother always said: "I never want to make that journey again." But surely Jacob would. He couldn't remember anything about being a baby on the ship. Surely he would want to know what it was like.

With a shake of her head, Anna dismissed him from her thoughts: "Probably he was fooling all the time."

She looked up from the road. On all sides of the valley the trees were turning color. The birch leaves were a light golden yellow, while the beech leaves were brownish red. Some of the maples were yellow, too, but others were orange or bright red. Here and there was an ash tree, with deep, purply-red leaves.

Every day after that, Father worked hard, cutting down trees at the edges of fields and grubbing out the stumps with the help of a team of oxen he borrowed from Mr. Cierzan. Every evening he and Franciszek came back to the house tired and weary. If they had managed to get rid of a particularly stubborn and deeply rooted stump, Father was in a good mood. He would sing the song about the wild hare:

Sedzi sobie zając pod miedza,
Pod miedza, pod miedza.
A myśliwy kedniem nie wiedzo,
Nie wiedzo, nie wiedzo.

Hare sits stilly, under the hedge,
Under the hedge, under the hedge.
And the handsome hunter sees him not,
Sees him not, sees him not.

When he came to the part about the hunter, Father would stalk around silently, pretending he had a trap in his arms. Anna, Anton and Julian ran and hid behind the rocker. As soon as Father finished singing he would sneak up to where they were hiding and pounce on them.

"Now I've got you in my trap!" he gloated when he caught one of them. When he caught Anna, she wriggled about until she got away and ran to hide again behind the rocker or under the table.

"Oh, that hare got away from me again!" cried Father. He turned to look at Mother. "Do you think I'll ever catch it?"

"I don't know," said Mother with a laugh.

But if Father had had a bad day and the stumps would not come out, he was in no mood to play and sing. Instead, he would complain to Mother.

"I tell you, we dug way under the roots and put the grappling hook as far down as we could, and we still couldn't get that devil of a stump out!"

"Hush, Frank!" cried Mother. She did not like it when Father talked that way.

"Jacob should be here to help you," said Anna. She was sure that then they could get the stump out.

"Oh, I guess Father and I can manage all right," said Franciszek, not wanting them to think he couldn't do a man's job. "We'll get it out tomorrow, you'll see."

"You bet we will," agreed Father.

"Just be thankful we have enough fields grubbed out so *you* don't have to go off for the winter to the lumber camps, too," Mother said to him. "I wouldn't like to think of going back to those days, living here all by myself."

"You were here by yourself?" Anna was surprised.

"Yes. Of course, Jacob and Franciszek were with me, but they were little then. Every winter we were here, alone."

"Weren't you scared?" asked Anna.

"Many times," agreed Mother. "After the second winter, Mrs. Walski was there, across the way, but sometimes the snowstorms were so bad, we couldn't even walk that short distance for weeks at a time." Mother stopped, as though she were thinking deeply about that time, but could not speak about it. Everyone else was silent, too.

"The worst times were when the wolves came," continued Mother after a while.

"Wolves!" cried Anna. Ever since that scary, stormy day when the threshing man had told them about the wolves nearby, Anna had been quite frightened. Even when they later heard that the pack of wolves had moved westward, and not in their direction, she was not completely convinced that someday she wouldn't meet up with a wolf.

"Yes, wolves," repeated Mother. "And bears. Many was the time we saw their tracks outside. Once there were claw marks, probably made by a bear, straight down the wood planks at the side of the door. It made me shiver in my shoes, I can tell you. Sometimes the wolves howled all night, so I could hardly sleep. But I still had to get up and milk Myszka. She was the only cow we had then."

"Our same Myszka, that we have now?" asked Anna. *Myszka* meant "Little Mouse," and they called her that because she was the color of a wee, gray mouse. But Anna could hardly believe Myszka was older than she was.

"No," said Mother. "This Myszka is the daughter of the one we had then. My, what a lot has happened since!"

Anna tried to picture Mother, alone in the house with Jacob and Franciszek. She tried to imagine the sound of the wolves, howling on the hills all around, and the scratching of the bear's claws. Chills went up and down her back, just thinking about it. How glad she was that

Father could stay with them every winter now! She didn't want him to leave, not ever.

That night, after they said their prayers, she crawled under the feather tick, between Mary and Pauline, and thought of their safe, snug house.

"I don't want to leave," she thought. "Not even to go to Poland. At least, not until I'm grown up."

But when she went to sleep, she dreamed that she was sailing away on a big ship, and all around her on the shore were wolves and bears, howling and clawing angrily because they could not reach her.

"You can't get me because I'm going to Poland!" she shouted at them in her dream, and then the ship went farther and farther and farther out onto the ocean.

Christmas Sun Balls

Advent came, and then Father didn't sing the hare song or some of the other funny songs he knew. Instead, he led them in special hymns and prayers. On the second Sunday of Advent, after dinner, the family was sitting quietly around the stove. Father snoozed in his rocking chair. Mother and Mary and Pauline were knitting and Anna was trying to learn how by watching them and practicing with her own needles and a knitted square. The long steel needles were awkward and hard to manage.

"Oh, no! I dropped another stitch," wailed Anna. She threw the knitting to the floor. "I don't want to knit anymore."

"Anna!" Mother's voice was stern. She did not have to say another word. Anna knew what she must do. She picked up the knitting with a sigh, and started to unravel the last row.

Suddenly, there was a sound of bells and stomping of feet outside the door. Father woke with a start.

"Whoever can that be?" he asked, looking at Mother.

"I can't imagine," replied Mother. Yet, she didn't look too surprised.

Father went to open the door and in stepped a group of young men, wearing funny sheepskins over their heads and shoulders. Only their eyes and mouths showed, through holes in the skins. One of them had a pair of ram's horns attached to the sheepskin, at the top of his head, and from his right hand swung a short, twisted rope. All of them carried small bundles of straw.

"Welcome, *gvjozdki!*" said Father.

"So that's what *gvjozdki* look like," thought Anna. She had heard Father and Mother and Jacob talk about them, but she had never seen them. In earlier years, the *gvjozdki* had always come while she was asleep.

The *gvjozdka* with the horns went to Mary and prodded her with a bunch of straw.

"Say your prayers," he growled. His voice seemed to come from deep within the sheepskin.

Mary held back a smile, knelt down, closed her eyes and began the Our Father. All the while she was praying, the other *gvjozdki* tickled her with straws and tried to make her laugh, but she kept on right to the end. When she had finished, one of the *gvjozdki* reached into a little sack and brought out a long stick of candy.

"Thank you!" said Mary and she went back to her place on the bench.

"Now you!" The horned *gvjozdka* poked Pauline in the ribs.

Pauline started to say a prayer, but as soon as she felt the straw tickling her neck, she had to giggle.

"So, is that the way you show respect?" growled the horned *gvjozdka*. He began to spank Pauline lightly, using the twisted rope. The more he spanked, the harder Pauline giggled. At last she came to the end of the prayer. The *gvjozdka* reached into his little sack and handed her only a short stick of candy.

"Oh," thought Anna. "I want a long stick. But how will I ever keep from laughing if they tickle me with the straw?" Then she remembered that Mary had closed her eyes. "That's what I'll do. I'll close my eyes and pretend I can't feel the straw."

While the *gvjozdki* teased and tickled Franciszek and Barney, Anna silently practiced saying her prayers, over and over, hoping she would not have to laugh or giggle.

"Your turn." The horned *gvjozdka* pointed to Anna. "Sing us a Christmas song."

Anna gaped at him. She loved to sing, but at that moment, not one word of one song came into her head. No matter how hard she tried, she couldn't think of one.

"*Lulajże, Jezuniu . . .*" whispered Mother from behind her, and as soon as Anna heard the words, she remembered the whole song. Closing her eyes, she began to sing:

Lulajże, Jezuniu, moja perełko,
Lulaj, ulubione me pieścidełko.
Lulajże, Jezuniu, lulajże, lulaj;
A ty go, Matuniu w płaczu utulaj.

Lullaby, little Jesus, my pearl,
Lullaby, my pet, my darling.

82

Lullaby, little Jesus, lullaby;
And you, His Mother, calm your weeping.

Her clear, sweet voice rose and fell. Verse after verse she sang, before she realized something. No one was tickling her or prodding her. Slowly she opened her eyes and looked up. Everyone was staring at her, listening intently, even the *gvjozdki*. When she came to the end of the song, there was complete silence in the room.

The *gvjozdka* with the sack cleared his throat. "Fine, fine!" he said, and handed her a big stick of candy, even longer than Mary's.

Anna wanted to start eating it right away, but Mother shook her head lightly.

"You must wait until Christmas," she said. "We'll put it away."

While the *gvjozdki* moved over to Anton, Anna clutched the candy. She wanted to hold it for as long as possible, even though she knew she must not eat it until Christmas.

At last the *gvjozdki* were finished. They didn't do anything to Julian because he was too little. Still, he got a stick of candy.

Just before they went out the door, the horned *gvjozdka* leaned over to Mother and whispered: "Mother said to tell you she's waiting to come and help as soon as you send the word."

"Yes, I'll send Franciszek," Mother whispered back.

Anna was standing nearby and heard them, but couldn't understand what it was all about. Did that mean-looking *gvjozdka* have a mother? And why would *his* mother come to help *her* mother? Was that how Mother would get her Christmas candy? Anna wondered and wondered, but no one explained.

A few days later Anna woke up and went to the kitchen in her nightgown. There, standing at the kitchen stove, was Mrs. Tushner. Mary and Pauline were just coming in with the milk.

"Let me have some of that to warm up for your mother," said Mrs. Tushner, in her low, accented voice.

Anna stared at her. She wanted to ask why she was there, but the words wouldn't come.

"Hurry and get dressed," said Mrs. Tushner. "Then you can go in and see your new baby brother."

Anna was astounded. "You mean the Indian woman came during the night and brought another baby?"

"Well, maybe," laughed Mrs. Tushner, "but I think it was the Baby Jesus who brought your little brother this time. He wanted some company for Christmas."

Anna still couldn't take it all in. Even later, when she tiptoed in to see the new baby, she could hardly believe that such a thing had happened yet again.

Mother smiled up at her from the bed, while she opened the blanket to show the baby's face.

"We're going to name him Alexander," she whispered.

For the next few days, Mother did not get up from her bed. Mrs. Tushner came each morning and told Mary and Pauline what they must do. Then one morning, they fixed up a seat by the fire for Mother, and she stayed there most of the day.

"I think we can manage on our own now," she said to Mrs. Tushner. "You must have so many things to get done before Christmas."

"Don't you worry. I'll get to it all," laughed Mrs. Tushner. "Besides, before long I'll be needed over at the Dorawas."

The day before Christmas was a Sunday, so they wrapped Alexander in many blankets and took him with them to be baptized after Mass. Aunt Bridget and her oldest son were the godparents.

As soon as the baptism was over, they bundled up and hurried home in the bobsled. There was still so much to do before tomorrow.

"Oh," said Anna as she thought of something. "Tonight is Christmas Eve. That means we'll go to church again, after it gets dark." She loved going to Midnight Mass. It was her favorite time of all the year.

During that whole day, even though it was a Sunday, Mother directed them in things to do. There was dinner to prepare, then wood to carry in—enough to last through the next day. After dinner the dishes had to be washed with special care. They polished the tin plates and cups until they were smooth and shiny. Before going out to feed and milk the cows, they set the supper table. First, they sprinkled straw over it, and then they placed Mother's linen cloth over the straw. When the plates and cups were set down, the straw made a crunchy sound.

"Don't forget to set the extra place," Mother reminded them. "You never know who will need shelter on Christmas Eve."

As they were about to sit down to eat, they heard bells and voices in the front yard.

"More *gvjozdki?*" asked Anna in surprise.

"Could be," said Father as he went to open the door. Sure enough, there stood two *gvjozdki* in sheepskins. One of them was covered with woolly fur from head to foot, but the other had a sheepskin only over his head and shoulders.

Once again the children had to show how nicely they could behave and say their prayers. But this time the *gvjozdka* with the sack did not bring out sticks of candy. Instead, he reached in and took out, one by one, round balls of reddish-gold and handed one to each of them. Anna did not know what to do with hers. She had never seen such a thing.

"Don't you know what it is?" asked Mother. "It's an orange, to eat. Smell it."

Anna held the orange to her nose. It smelled so tangy it made her nostrils prickle.

"That's the smell of the sun," said Mother. "These oranges have been growing on trees, far away, where the sun is always shining. They soaked up so much sun they finally turned the same color. We'll eat them tomorrow."

Anna was so intent on smelling her orange, she didn't even notice that the *gvjozdki* had left.

Suddenly, there was a stamping at the door and then it opened again. There stood Jacob, tall and smiling. Anna ran to him and started to tell him about the *gvjozdki*.

"Oh, Jacob, they came twice! First they gave us candy sticks and then they brought us these . . . these . . . sun balls!" She could not remember the word "orange."

"That's a good way to describe them," said Jacob with a smile.

"I wish you had been here, Jacob. Maybe they would have given one to you. There was even one for Mother and one for Father."

"It just so happens I did meet up with a *gvjozdka*," said Jacob. "And look!" He pulled an orange from his pocket. "I got one, too."

They put the oranges in a bowl in the center of the table, where they could look at them while they ate. Anna forked the smoked carp and potatoes with cream gravy into her mouth, but hardly tasted them. All she could think of was the candy and oranges that they would eat tomorrow.

"I wonder what the sun balls will taste like! Maybe," she thought, "they will be sweeter than the candy."

But next morning, when Mother let them eat their oranges, Anna gulped in surprise.

"It's sweet, but not sweeter than candy," she thought, as the tingly juice slid down her throat. She couldn't make up her mind what the orange tasted like. She wasn't even sure she liked it as much as the candy.

"Do you like your orange?" asked Jacob.

"I think so," said Anna. "It tastes like . . . like Christmas!" And then she was sure that she did like oranges, and wanted one for Christmas every year.

Train Scare

Jacob stayed only for Christmas Eve and Christmas Day. Then he had to go back to his job at the lumber camp. Father and Franciszek continued to work at the edge of the fields. Now that the ground was frozen, they could no longer pull out stumps. Instead, they snaked out the logs from the trees they had cut down and loaded them onto the big bobsled. When there were six big logs on the bobsled, Father would take it to Mr. Bortle's sawmill in Dodge.

After the logs were sawed into lumber, Father took the planks made from four logs and loaded them back onto the bobsled. The other planks stayed at the sawmill for Mr. Bortle to sell. They were the payment Father had to make for getting his logs sawed.

"I'll get that new barn yet," said Father as he piled the planks neatly on top of the low stack of weathered boards that he had started to build up last year. He wanted to build a bigger barn, out of stone and boards, not logs like the one they had now.

It was hard work loading the logs onto the sled. Each log was so heavy, even Father could not lift one end more than a few inches off the ground. They chained one log at a time to the whippletree, and then the two teams of horses had to pull steady and hard in order to slide it through the snow, up the slanting wooden skid and onto the bobsled. Sometimes it took all morning to get the load placed and balanced just right.

Anna wanted to see how they took the logs off again and made them into boards, but Father had never said she might go along, and she must not ask.

"Go and see how soon your father will be coming in for dinner," Mother told Anna, late one morning.

Hardly had Anna stepped outside, when Father drove up with a loaded bobsled. It was a half hour before noon.

"Can we have a quick bite to eat now?" he asked. "Then we'll be on our way."

"Oh, dear! Dinner's not ready yet," answered Mother. "But I can always put out some bread and butter and milk."

While Father and Franciszek went in to eat quickly, Anna eyed the pile of logs on the bobsled.

"That must feel high and mighty, riding up on top of the logs," she thought. She glanced around to see if anyone was looking. "I'll just climb up part way," she said to herself.

Grasping one of the side poles that held the logs in place, she swung up and onto the first log. Then she moved up to the next log.

"It's not really so high," she thought, and moved up to the top log. Now she could look down on everything. It did feel high, and scary. Carefully, she inched her way forward to the front of the log. It was hard to move without snagging her dress or shawl on the rough bark.

At last she was sitting at the front of the logs, where Father usually sat to drive the horses. Anna pretended she was guiding the two teams down to the road: "Come along now. Nice and easy does it."

Out of the corner of her eye she saw that Father had wound the reins around one of the lowest logs.

"It wouldn't hurt if I just held them," she thought. "I won't snap them or move them." She was about to reach down and unwind the reins when Father and Franciszek came out the door.

"What do you think you're doing up there?" asked Franciszek crossly.

"So you'd like to take a ride on the logs, would you?" Father's voice was surprised, but not angry.

Anna nodded her head. She was afraid to say anything.

"Well, I don't see what harm could come if you ride along for once," said Father. "Franciszek, run in and tell your mother Anna's going with us."

Franciszek did not like that at all. He stomped back into the house, and in a minute, both he and Mother appeared at the door.

"Oh, Frank, do you think she should go?" asked Mother.

"Can't see the harm in it," replied Father.

"But the men. They're so rough. And she hasn't had any dinner."

"I'm not hungry," said Anna quickly. "Not the least bit." How could she be hungry when she was so excited! It would be the first time she went near the sawmill when it was working. Maybe she would hear some swearing—not a lot, but enough to know what it sounded like.

For a moment, Father looked as though he might change his mind, but before he could, Mother had turned back into the house. She came out carrying a thick slice of buttered bread.

"Here, at least take this along to eat," she said. "Are you bundled up enough?"

Anna took off her mitten and reached for the bread.

"It's not very cold out," she protested. In fact, she was flushed and warm.

"We won't be long," said Father. "This load will be off in no time." With a flick of the wrist he twitched the reins and signaled the horses that it was time to be off.

Down to the valley road they slid. Father held the horses back so they would not take the hill too fast. The late February sun was not as strong as the summer sun, but because there was no wind, it warmed the cold air so that it felt crisp and refreshing instead of stinging and biting. In and around the winding curves they glided. The valley road was so level it seemed no effort for the horses to pull the heavily loaded sled.

"Aren't you glad we brought her along?" Father said to Franciszek. Franciszek still seemed to be annoyed that Anna had been allowed to come with them.

"She'll be a big help when we have to push this load up Mrozek's hill," continued Father.

Franciszek and Anna stared at him as though he were

a stranger saying crazy things. Then they both burst out laughing.

"You're a fine one," said Father as he poked Franciszek in the ribs. "Won't even help me to have a little teasing fun."

"You can't fool me about that," laughed Anna. "I know you could never push this big load up such a steep hill." She and Franciszek joked and laughed as they rode along. Now he was in a good mood, just like Father.

On the long, level stretch before Mrozek's hill, Father urged the horses into a smooth steady speed. They kept it up for more than half way up the hill, but then they began to slow down. Father and Franciszek jumped off.

"You stay up there," Father ordered Anna. "Hang on tight."

The double team of horses strained hard, pulling with all their strength, while Father guided them and Franciszek pushed from behind. Anna clung to the top log, now tilted far backward because of the slant of the hill. She was afraid to look anywhere except straight ahead.

"Come on, Lord and Lady! Come on, Star and Brownie! You can do it!" Anna called out to the horses. And then they were at the top.

"Well done!" shouted Father. He let the horses rest for a moment, and then kept them at a slow walk for about a mile.

The rest of the road to Dodge was easy. Only slight ups and downs appeared in the road, enough to give Anna a tickly feeling inside as the horses sped along. Soon they came to the edge of town and once again Father slowed the horses to a walk. They passed the first row of houses and turned to cross the railroad tracks.

Suddenly, right at the edge of the tracks, the bobsled

came to an abrupt stop. Father and Franciszek almost lost their balance, and Anna was pitched so far forward her nose scraped the log on which she was sitting.

"What's the matter there?" asked Father as he peered down and tried to calm the horses at the same time. "Jump down and have a look, Frank."

Franciszek quickly climbed down from his perch and went to the front of the bobsled's runners. The horses were nervously prancing and stamping so he could not get too close.

"Looks like one of the runners is stuck on the outside rail," said Franciszek. He tried to stoop down and reach in to brush the snow away so he could see, but each time he got close, Brownie kicked up her heels.

"Go to the front and hold her bridle," ordered Father. "I'll see if I can reach down and push the runner free."

In the same moment that Franciszek started walking toward Brownie's head, a high, piercing whistle echoed through the countryside from far down the tracks.

"The train!" shrieked Franciszek. The horses pranced more nervously than before.

Quickly Father turned to Anna. "Jump off! And stand far back."

Guiding herself by the left side pole, Anna slithered down the pile of logs as fast as she could. As she stepped to the edge of the sled, her dress caught in a crack on one of the logs.

"Hurry!" shouted Father. "Tear it free!"

Anna pulled at her skirt and heard it rip as it tore loose. Then she ran backward, as far away from the bobsled as she could get.

Hooo-eeee! Again, the train whistle sounded, this time much closer.

Brownie reared up on her hind legs, bumping against

93

the bobsled. Anna saw it move backward a bit.

"It's free!" cried Franciszek. "The runner's free!"

Father quickly calmed the horses and pulled them sharply to the left, swinging the bobsled up and over the tracks, safely to the other side. Just as he did so, the train came into view, chuffing and puffing. It passed the crossing, going slower and slower, until finally it came to a full stop at the station, farther down the road.

By now a small crowd of people had gathered on both sides of the tracks. Everything had happened in such a short time, and Anna had been so scared, she had not noticed where they came from. She looked fearfully across to the spot where her father stood.

"You can cross now," he called out to her.

Swallowing back a sob, she ran to Father and Franciszek who were talking excitedly to the crowd.

"I don't know what happened," Father said. "The runners have never done that before." He leaned down to show them that neither of the runners was bent or split.

They talked for a few more minutes, letting the scared feeling gradually work its way out of their insides. Then, without getting up on the logs, Father picked up the reins and directed the horses over to the sawmill, close by the river. Anna and Franciszek walked slowly behind.

Father helped the men unload. They put one of the logs on the platform leading to the tall headsaw with its jagged teeth. Anna stood back and watched as the big, noisy headsaw bit into the side of the log.

"See that first slab? It's mostly bark, so they won't put it up to the edging saw," explained Franciszek.

But the rest of the slabs were passed up and to the side where the edging saw cut away the two rough edges. Then the slabs became thick planks of lumber, even and straight on all sides.

Thick clouds of sawdust spit out in all directions and settled beneath the saws. Every few minutes, a boy stepped up and raked it away.

When the boards were ready, Father and Franciszek carried them to the bobsled. They also filled a few sacks with sawdust and put them on top of the boards. Then it was time to return home.

Anna's heart thumped as they approached the railroad crossing, but this time the sled's runners passed over as smoothly as butter being spread on bread.

"Well," said Father as they settled down for the ride home, "we have to thank our guardian angels. They were watching out for us today all right."

Silently, Anna said a prayer of thanks. She was not sure she was sorry or glad they had had such a scare. But if such exciting things were bound to happen, then she was grateful she had a guardian angel to watch over her.

The School Burns Down

One morning in early March, Anna was awakened by a loud pounding on the door.

"Hold your horses, I'm coming!" Father called out loudly from the next room.

Pauline sat up in bed. "What is going on?" she whispered.

"I don't know," whispered Anna back. "Someone has been knocking at the door."

"What could anyone want at this hour?" asked Pauline. "It's not even light yet."

"Let's go see," suggested Anna. She didn't want to go alone, but if Pauline went with her, she wouldn't be scared.

Under the feather tick, Mary turned over in bed, and didn't even look up at them. They hopped out of bed and crept to the curtain that hung over their doorway. Peeking around it, they could see Father at the door, inviting young August Kaldunski into the house.

"No, I can't come in," answered August hurriedly. "You're supposed to come quickly. The school is on fire!"

Without another word, Father pulled on his boots, slipped on his coat and cap and went out the door.

Mother stepped from behind the curtain leading to her bedroom. She was still in her nightgown.

"What are you girls doing up?" she asked as soon as she saw Pauline and Anna.

"We heard the commotion and wondered what it was," answered Pauline.

"Seems the school is on fire," said Mother, shaking her head. "What next?" She looked at the stove. "I might as well stay up and make some breakfast." She opened the damper, lifted the lid, scraped away the ashes covering the last few coals and put a handful of wood shavings and kindling on top of the embers. They flared up quickly and soon she could add a few sticks of wood. Before long, the fire was roaring.

Anna and Pauline stood close to it, holding out their hands to catch the warmth. Mother left them there and went into her bedroom to get dressed. In a few moments she came out again.

"Back to bed with you," she scolded mildly. "Or else get dressed."

Quickly they ran to their bedroom, snatched up their clothes and raced back to the warmth of the stove. There they put on their flannel petticoats and undershirts, and over them their thick woolen dresses.

"If the school burns down, does that mean we don't have to go any more?" Pauline asked Mother. She and Mary had only started to attend school that winter and neither of them liked it at all.

"There are too many big boys and they always torment us," Mary had said as she and her sister returned home after the first day. "And besides, I can't understand a word Mr. Batcheller is saying. I don't like talking in English."

"Just the same, you have to go," Mother had insisted. "At least until you learn to read and write."

Anna was glad Mother didn't think she was old enough yet to go to school. The idea of having to figure out all those English words was alarming.

Suddenly, there was a thump! thump! thump! on the ladder as Franciszek came stepping down.

"What's everybody doing up so early?" he asked with a yawn.

"The school is burning down," said Pauline excitedly.

Franciszek grinned at her, realizing what that meant. He didn't mind school as much as the two girls, because he was big enough to hold his own with the boys. Still, he didn't like getting all those raps on the knuckles from Mr. Batcheller, and only because he couldn't make sense out of the funny way English words kept changing their sounds.

Mother started cooking the *kasha* made of buckwheat groats, while the children talked about the burning school and what would happen next. When the *kasha* was ready, she ladled it into the tin bowls and they ate it with warm clabbered milk left from the day before.

"Shall I hitch up Lord and Lady and go help them?"

asked Franciszek as soon as he had finished eating.

"Better not," answered Mother. "We should hear soon if they caught it in time."

Not long after they finished breakfast, Father came back.

"That's the end of *that* school," he said with finality. "It was over before we got there. Those logs went up like matchsticks once they caught on fire. They managed to save the books and most of the desks, but where they'll put them is a big question. Kaldunski has no extra room in his house or barn."

"It's a mercy it happened at night when no one was there," said Mother.

"Does that mean we won't go to school anymore?" asked Franciszek.

"Not for today, anyway," answered Father. "Tonight all the men are going to meet here to decide what to do."

That evening, as soon as chores were done, wagons and bobsleds started arriving from both directions. Soon the kitchen was full of people, chattering and discussing the situation. Anna and her sisters were supposed to go to bed, but they listened from behind the curtain.

"I say we should tear down what's left of the old school and build in the same spot," suggested Mr. Kaldunski.

"Wait just a moment, there," protested Mr. Olszewski. "It seems to me that it would be better if we built closer to the center of the valley. Then it wouldn't be so far for those living all the way in."

"A good idea," chimed in Mr. Dorawa. "Then John would only have to go half the distance."

"But what about *our* children?" asked Mr. Moga. "I don't want them having to go all the way around and into the valley." The Mogas lived at the top of Kaldunski's hill.

"Ours would have a long way to walk, too," said Mr. Wasztok. "I'm satisfied with the school staying where it is!"

"Well, now," said Father. "I tend to agree with

Olszewski here. This is the Latsch Valley School. It should be *in* the valley. It always seemed kind of unfair to me that our young ones have to walk so much farther. It's a shame the school had to burn down, but I say we should take advantage of that and find a new spot for it, closer to most of us."

"Yes, and you probably were the one that set fire to it," mumbled one of the men. Anna could not tell who it was, but she was shocked. How could anyone suggest such a thing? She peeked around the edge of the curtain.

Father was standing up, looking angry and disgusted. He looked ready to fight anyone who repeated such a suggestion.

Suddenly Mr. Tushner stood up. "Look here, neighbors. No need to get so hot under the collar. My farm is just about midway between the two ends of the valley. How would it be if I gave a piece of land, just off the road, for a new school?"

"That's a good idea!"

"That certainly seems fair to all." The men all nodded their agreement. It seemed a good solution.

"Fine, that settles it."

"Well and good," said Mr. Kaldunski, "but what do we do until the new school can be built? I've got those desks sitting in my front yard and they can't stay there much longer or they'll be no good to us."

"What about that house on the Majkowski place?" suggested Mr. Dorawa. "He doesn't intend to come out with his family until planting time. He'd probably let us have the school there for a few months."

"Let's ask him if we can use it. Who's going to town next?" asked Mr. Kaldunski.

While the men discussed setting up the temporary

school, and plans for building the new one, Pauline turned to Anna.

"Guess we won't get out of school after all," she moaned.

"Maybe they won't let them use the house," answered Anna.

"No such chance," said Mary. "There'll be school, you'll see."

But she was wrong, because in a few days there were such bad snowstorms, no one could move far from the house, not even Father and the boys. In the evenings they sat around the stove, trying to keep warm.

One evening Father brought out his leather money purse from the secret place where he kept it hidden. He counted out all the money that was in it and sighed.

"I'll just about make it," he said. "After the fifty dollars I promised toward finishing off the church, I'll have about ten dollars left to put toward the school, and that's what we're each supposed to give. I hope you won't be needing much of anything until the crops come in this summer, because we won't have the cash for it, and you know I don't like to buy on credit."

"Couldn't we ask Father Snigourski to let us delay the church payment?" asked Mother, with a worried look. She didn't like to be without money in the house.

"I promised it to him for Easter, and you know that when I give my word, I keep it. My word is Verdun," said Father firmly.

Anna had heard Father say that many times before, but she didn't know what it meant, exactly. Father seemed in a talkative mood, so it was a good time to ask him.

"Why do you always say that, Father? What is Verdun?"

"When I was young, in Poland, I was studying with the priests," answered Father. "I thought I might like to be a priest myself someday."

"A priest? Like Father Snigourski?" exclaimed Anna. She and all the other children looked with amazement at Father. They had never heard him mention this before.

"If Father was a priest, he wouldn't have any children," thought Anna. She was so overcome by this thought, she almost forgot about Verdun. But Father had not, so he continued his story.

"The priests told us all about the early days of history," he explained. "And Verdun was one of the places they talked about. I'm not sure myself where it is, but anyway, in that city the grandsons of the great emperor Charlemagne signed a treaty, the Treaty of Verdun. They didn't always like to live up to it, but they had given their word. And so when I give my word, it's like that Treaty of Verdun. I always keep it."

"Father makes it sound so grand," thought Anna. "That's the kind of thing I'd like to study in school—not those hard English words." She felt sure that if she went back to Poland, she would learn all about Verdun, and emperors and kings and queens.

Bismarck's Boots

"Say, Frank, I have a newspaper from Prussia. Do you want to read it?" A man stopped Father as they were coming out from church one Sunday late in May.

"Yes, I would like to read what's going on there," answered Father.

The man went to his wagon and pulled a folded newspaper out from a sack. He handed it to Father.

"You can pass it on to Dorawa when you're finished. He likes to read the news, too."

Father thanked the man and then he and Mother moved slowly among the groups of people, chatting about the good spring weather, and how fine it had been for spring planting. The children followed along behind until they reached their wagon.

Mr. Rudnik and his family came strolling up. His wagon and team were hitched right next to Father's.

"Wait a minute, Frank. I have something for you." Mr. Rudnik reached into a corner of his wagon and pulled out a Polish newspaper from Chicago. "I got this last week. We finished reading it so I thought you'd like to have a look."

"It never rains but it pours," laughed Father. "Andrew Losinski just gave me a newspaper from Prussia. Well, it will be good to get all that news for a change. I'll give them both to Dorawa after I finish reading them. He'll know where to pass them on."

As soon as dinner was over, Father brought out the newspapers. First he opened the one from Prussia. He read silently for a while and then began to read aloud. Only Mother could understand, because she could speak German and even read it a little.

Slowly and carefully Father sounded out the words. Anna could not make out what they meant. She knew how to count from one to ten in German, and there were other words she had learned from hearing Father buy things at the store in Dodge. But these were long and difficult words he was reading. She had never heard them before. Father kept repeating one of them in almost every sentence.

At last he put aside that paper and picked up the Polish one. It was called the *Gazeta Polska*. Now, when Father read aloud to Mother, they could all understand. Anna always got a chill up and down her back when she heard about the things happening in Chicago: fires that burned down many homes and buildings, because they were so close together; runaway horses that trampled children in the streets; robbers who stole things in broad daylight.

Suddenly, Anna heard Father saying that same word he had been repeating from the Prussian paper: Bismarck.

"'The forthcoming retirement of Bismarck is looked upon by the Vatican as an opportune moment for resuming negotiations between church and state.'" With a shake of the paper, Father stopped reading.

"Bah! What are they writing about? That Bismarck— he'll never retire."

Anna looked up in surprise. Something seemed to be upsetting Father and making him angry.

"Who is Bismarck?" she asked.

"He's a sly old fox, that's who he is."

"Frank, don't get yourself excited for nothing," pleaded Mother. Then she turned to Anna. "Bismarck is the head of the Prussian government," she explained.

Anna still could not understand what made Father so upset.

"When you were in the Prussian army, did you meet Bismarck?" asked Franciszek.

Father looked at him intently. Then he slapped his thigh and laughed.

"I did meet his boots. And how! I got to know his boots very well, every crease and corner of them!" Once again, Father laughed and stared off to one corner of the room, as though he could see something far away, right through the wall.

They all looked at him expectantly. At last he glanced up and saw their questioning faces.

"So you want me to tell you about the time I got in trouble as a soldier, is that it?" Slowly, Father got up from his chair. When he told a story, he liked to pace up and down and act out certain parts.

"Well, I was just a young fellow then, and I hadn't

been in the army a year. My mother and father were both dead. I asked permission to go back home and see how Bridget and my brother John were doing. They were living with our uncle and aunt. Tom Kukowski—he was in the same company I was—he begged me to stop off and give his mother some of his money, and I foolishly promised him I would. I only had five days' leave and it took a lot of walking to get to Uncle Joseph's place. As soon as I got there, I knew I would be late getting back to the army post if I stopped off to deliver Tom's money. But there was nothing else I could do. I had given him my word."

"And your word is Verdun, isn't that right, Father?" interrupted Anna.

"That it is," agreed Father with a nod, and then he continued his story.

"Just as I thought, it took me quite a while to get to the Kukowskis' home, and then I had to turn around and make the long trip back. It was raining and the roads and fields were thick with mud. Up to my knees it was, in some places. It took me almost two days of walking, and instead of getting to the army post at six, like I was supposed to, I got there near midnight. There was a foggy drizzle, but I could see a couple of other soldiers from another company were just behind me, also getting in late. They were singing and laughing as though they hadn't a care in the world. We tried to slip in the gate without being seen, but an officer standing just inside called out 'Who goes there?' so I went up to him and saluted."

Here Father stood up straight and saluted in the direction of the door, as though he could see a military officer there:

"'Gemeiner Pellowski. Kompagnie B. Dritte Bataillon. Erstes Landwehr Regiment. Erste Infanterie Brigade.'" He sounded out each phrase in German and clicked his heels. Then he quickly turned around and pretended he was the officer:

"'Why are you returning so late?'"

Father turned and once again he was acting like a twenty-year-old soldier, scared and shivering:

"'I went home and I . . . I . . . I couldn't get back . . . uh . . . uh . . . in time,'" he stuttered.

109

"'Couldn't get back in time, you say? Don't they have a clock in the tavern? Or are you so tipsy you can't tell the time?'" Father's voice was strict and firm, like that of a general. "'Into the lockup with you. We'll see what your company captain has to say about it in the morning.'"

"'Bb . . . b . . . b . . . but I wasn't with them!'" Father shivered and shook again, as though he were still facing that strict, mean officer.

"'Guard, off to the lockup with these men, and be quick about it.'"

Father stopped acting out his story and turned to face his family. "They did put me in the lockup, too! I was too scared to explain that I was coming back from a home leave and hadn't been drinking with the others. But the next day, the captain could see they were not from my company.

"'Those tipplers will be put on bread and water for a day,' he said, 'but what am I going to do with you? We can't have every soldier taking his time and coming back when he pleases. We must have discipline.'

"I didn't say a thing. We learned early on that the less you said in the army, the better you got on. So, after looking me over a bit, the captain finally told me he was going to turn me over to the orderly. A group of officers from the Life Guards had come in, and they needed their gear cleaned and polished. So they set me to cleaning up the saddles and the boots and polishing them until they shone. Half the morning I rubbed and buffed until you could see your face in that shiny leather.

"It had been raining again, and the military yard was filled with puddles of water. Along came one of the men from the officers' quarters and asked me for the boots. I gave them to him and he took off, running across the yard in the light rain. Wouldn't you know, he dropped a pair of boots right in a deep, muddy puddle. So back he came to me with them.

"'You'd better do these over. Lieutenant Bismarck, he's a fussy one.'

"I polished those boots a second time and took them myself to the officers' quarters. There they all were, sitting and drinking coffee and joking about Bismarck's missing boots. He put them on as soon as I brought them, and the officers got up to leave.

"They were standing in the yard, waiting for their horses, when a coach and four horses came through the gate. It was the *Kommandant* and I figured he wouldn't be too happy to see all those officers from the Life Guards just standing around. He didn't like it when they arrived like that, without warning. We had heard him complaining before that he didn't have time to waste catering to a bunch of officers with nothing but time on their hands.

"Anyway, the coach came rolling into the yard, and veered off right behind the spot where the officers were standing. Whoosh! those coach wheels tore through the deep puddle, and dirty water went splashing in a spray all along the backsides of those officers. Bismarck—he got the worst of it. Not only his boots needed cleaning now. The seat of his pants looked as though he hadn't made it to the outhouse in time."

"Did he get mad?" asked Anna with a giggle, as Father paused while they all laughed.

"He was in a fury. He tore up to that coach driver and was starting to swear at him when out of the coach stepped the *Kommandant*. They stared at each other for a moment, and then came the bowing and scraping and excusing:

"'Good morning, *Herr Kommandant*. I did not see it was your coach.'

"'Good morning, *Herr Oberst*. I trust that my coach-man has not harmed you in any way.'

"'Not at all, *Herr Kommandant*. I should have stepped aside.'

"'I'll see to it that my driver is more careful in the future, *Herr Oberst*.'"

Father acted out the exchange of polite speeches and then laughed.

"You should have seen them, trying to be polite when they looked as though they would prefer to be at each other's throats. It gave us a good laugh that evening, back in the barracks. But it also gave *me* the job of cleaning Bismarck's boots again, and some of the other officers' boots as well. I was mighty sick of boot cleaning, I can tell you, because they wouldn't let me stop for dinner. I had to wait until evening to get something to eat."

"Couldn't you sneak away and get something, like a crust of bread?" asked Anna.

"Never! Not in the Prussian army. There were strict rules and they always knew where we were and what we were supposed to be doing."

"Well, I want to go to Poland someday, but I'll stay far away from Prussia," said Anna firmly. "I don't think I'd like it there."

At that, Father and Mother laughed heartily.

"What's so funny?" asked Anna, but they didn't explain and only laughed harder.

"It must be because they think I'll never manage to get there," thought Anna. "But they'll see, someday I'll go to Poland."

Name Day

June was a busy month. The meadows were thick with clover and timothy and other grasses that the cows and sheep and horses liked to munch on. The bees and butterflies fluttered and swooped, hurrying to get as much nectar as they could before the hay was cut and dried.

Before long, the small loft in the barn was filled and then two haystacks were heaped high near the barn. And still there was more hay.

"I do believe we have enough to sell a load or two," gloated Father. "That will put some cash back in the purse."

The hot, dry days continued into July, and they

brought in every bundle of hay they could find. Father sold two loads to the owner of the livery stable in Arcadia.

Now there was corn to cultivate and thistles and weeds to be pulled out of the wheat and oats fields. Also, Anna had a new job: taking care of the goslings. Mother had "borrowed" one setting from Mrs. Glenzinski. She would pay it back next year when the young geese started to lay their first eggs.

Every day Anna had to look for nettles and pick them, even though the leaves prickled and itched. Pauline helped her chop them, and then scattered them in front of the goslings, who gobbled the nettles up as though they were the tastiest of delicacies.

By late July, they could ease up on their long working days. Everything was growing well and the weeds were under control.

"Let's have a name day surprise for Mother," suggested Mary one Sunday as the girls were sitting under an apple tree, lazily passing the afternoon.

"Oh, yes! Let's!" agreed Anna. Mother's name day was on July 26, that Thursday.

"We could make her a special cake," proposed Pauline.

"And a flower wreath, to wear in her hair," added Anna.

"But she'd see us," said Mary. "She's always around the house these days."

"We could go to Cierzan's house," suggested Anna. "Julia and Frances would help us. I'm sure Mrs. Cierzan would let us make all the things there."

"We'd need some ribbons," said Mary. "Do you have any extra ones, Pauline?"

Pauline gave her an embarrassed look. "No, I only

have the two that I wear on Sunday. Mother would never let me use those for a wreath. Those were a present from my godparents, don't you remember?" She didn't mention the two pretty blue ribbons she had carelessly lost one Sunday because she had forgotten to take them off before she went to get the cows.

Anna jumped up suddenly and turned to Mary.

"You go ask Father if he'll buy a few ribbons. I heard him say he was taking the last load of hay to Arcadia this week. Pauline and I will run over to Mrs. Cierzan right now and ask her if we can make the cake there."

Mary hesitated because she knew Father had been worried about having no money. Then she remembered that he had already sold two loads of hay. Surely he could spare a few cents for ribbons for Mother.

"I'll do it," she agreed, jumping up.

Pauline and Anna set off for a visit to the Cierzan place, after telling Mother that was where they were going. When they came back with Mrs. Cierzan's promise to cooperate, they could see that Mary, too, had good news, because she was smiling. But there was no time to share it, because Mother was giving them errands to run or jobs to do.

That evening, in bed, the three girls whispered their news.

"What did Father say?"

"He'll get us some ribbons tomorrow or Tuesday, whichever day he goes to Arcadia. What color do we want?"

"Blue," said Anna.

"Red," said Pauline.

"I'll tell him to get some of each color," said Mary. "In fact, he should get as many colors as they have. Then

Mother's wreath will look like a rainbow."

"Mrs. Cierzan said you can make the cake there. She had flour and butter, but you must bring eggs and honey. She'll send Julia over with an errand on Wednesday, so that we'll be sure to get away without Mother suspecting something."

On Tuesday, Father went to Arcadia and when he returned, there was much frantic motioning and talking to distract Mother's attention while Mary brought in a large package wrapped in brown paper.

"That package is awfully big to hold only ribbons," whispered Anna that evening as they were going to bed.

"Shhhh! It's another surprise for Mother, from Father. I promised I wouldn't tell." Mary was bursting with the secret but she would say no more.

The next day, after dinner, Julia Cierzan appeared at their door.

"Good afternoon, Mrs. Pellowski. Mother would like to know if Mary and Pauline and Anna can come over for a few hours to help us. We're washing and drying wool, and she'd like to get it all spread out to dry this afternoon."

"Of course," replied Mother. "I'll even come, if you think she can use the help. Julian and Alexander could keep out of mischief playing with your little sisters."

"She didn't say anything about you. I don't think you're supposed to come," blurted out Julia.

Mother gave her a funny look and then turned to her daughters.

"Off you go, then, girls. Be back in time for chores."

"Do you think she suspects?" asked Pauline as they raced down to the road.

"I hope I didn't give it away," said Julia. "I didn't know what to say when she offered to come."

"I thought your mouth would fall below your chin," laughed Mary. "But don't worry. If she suspects something, it doesn't matter. She's sure to see some eggs missing later on, and if she looks in the honey jar she'll wonder how it got so low all of a sudden. I managed to hide them both down by the road this morning. They're under that bush."

They lifted out a cloth with a half-dozen eggs and a small crockery jar with honey in it.

"Where are the ribbons?" asked Anna.

"You'll see," was all Mary would say.

The moment they arrived, Mrs. Cierzan took over.

"Mary, you can help me with the cake, and the rest of you girls must go out and gather the flowers."

"I want to see the ribbons," said Anna stubbornly. "Then I'll know what kind of flowers to pick."

"All right, silly! Here are the ribbons!" Mary thrust open the cloth holding the eggs, and everyone squealed with delight. Coiled up on the eggs, like the most colorful snakes in the world, were many different ribbons, in all the colors of the rainbow.

"We could make a wreath of ribbons," laughed Mrs. Cierzan.

"Oh, no! We must use flowers *and* ribbons," Anna insisted.

"Go out and pick them then. I have morning glories and nasturtiums alongside the house but they won't last if you pick them today. Better find some daisies and asters. And there was some Indian paintbrush last time I looked in the back field, right at the edge of the woods."

Anna and Julia and Pauline set off for the woods and fields. For almost two hours they roamed up and down, plucking and gathering all the wild flowers they could find.

They came back to the house dusty, tired and thirsty for a drink of cool spring water. Mrs. Cierzan had just taken two large honey cakes out of the oven. It smelled so heavenly in the kitchen, Anna almost forgot her thirst.

"We'll just have time to get the wreath ready and then we must go back," said Mary. She twisted several strands of wire into a circle.

"Let me try it on you, Anna."

"But my head is much smaller than Mother's."

"I know that. We'll use this circle as the pattern and make hers bigger." Mary set the wire circlet aside and twisted another one into shape. Anna did not notice but Julia slyly slipped away with the first wire circle.

Mary began to fasten the ribbons onto one portion of the larger wire circle. When she had five of them attached, she held up the wire wreath and the ribbons floated and danced as they unfurled.

"Are you sure that's all the ribbons?" asked Anna. "It looked like there were more before."

"If we put any more on, there won't be room for flowers," said Mary. "Let's start."

They took turns weaving the stems of flowers in and out of the wires. All around went a row of daisies, and then another. Entwined between them were the colored flowers. Soon there was not a space left to be filled. Mary held the wreath up and they looked at it in wonder. While they had been working on it, they had not seen how lovely it was. Now that it was complete, they could hardly believe their own hands had made it.

"I wish we could take it and put it on Mother's head right now," whispered Anna.

"Better wait for the morning," said Mrs. Cierzan gently.

"But will the flowers last?"

"We'll sprinkle them with cool water. And if some wilt, we'll replace them in the morning. See, you picked enough flowers for several wreaths."

"I'll come and help you," offered Anna. "I can sneak away after I get water from the spring."

"Better not," said Mrs. Cierzan. "Julia and Frances and I can bring everything over. We'll come right after breakfast."

Anna was so excited that evening, she didn't think she could fall asleep. But she did. The night went by and then she was up again, doing her usual tasks.

At the breakfast table, everyone looked at Mother. She stared back at them, a little crossly.

"I don't know what's going on, but *someone* could at least wish me a Happy Name Day."

The boys dutifully responded: "Happy Name Day, Mother."

Father and the girls said nothing.

"I wish the Cierzans would come," thought Anna. She could hardly bear the suspense.

As they were getting up from the table, they heard the sound of faint singing coming from the direction of the road. It grew louder and louder.

"It sounds like a procession at church," laughed Mother nervously. "Has Father Snigourski decided to come all the way here to celebrate St. Anna's Day?"

"Let's go see," said Father with a smile.

They filed out of the house and waited in the yard. The singing grew louder. Soon the procession reached the top of the hill and they could see it as well as hear it.

In front came Frances Cierzan, bearing the lovely wreath. The colored ribbons fluttered and danced in the breeze like a rainbow that had been separated into strips.

Next came Mrs. Cierzan, carefully balancing one of the cakes. Behind her toddled little Josephine and the baby, Tillie, who was not yet two. Clutched in their tiny fists were nosegays of flowers.

Following the Cierzans came Mrs. Walski and her two daughters, and Mrs. Jaszewski with her daughter Agnes. They each carried either a honey cake or a bouquet of flowers.

But last of all came the biggest surprise, for Anna. It was Julia Cierzan, and she was carrying a second wreath with ribbons, smaller than the first one, but just as pretty.

Laughing and singing, the procession moved up to where Mother was standing.

"Happy Name Day," said Frances as she placed the first wreath on Mother's head.

Then Julia stepped up. "Happy Name Day," she repeated as she put the second wreath on Anna's head.

Anna was speechless. Of course, she had known it was her name day, too, but in the excitement of planning the surprise for Mother, she had forgotten all about herself.

"There's another surprise," cried Mary, and she ran in to get the large brown parcel.

"Open it carefully," she said, handing it to Mother.

From inside the wrappings of paper and cloth, Mother took out a large white china plate. It was so white that Anna was blinded by the sun that glanced off it, but when she was able to look closer, she noticed, all around the edge, a painted wreath of tiny flowers, similar to the ones in the wreath around Mother's head. She had never seen such a beautiful plate before. Mother looked happily over at Father, who was beaming.

"And now your surprise," laughed Mrs. Walski as she thrust a package into Anna's hands. "Careful! It could break, too."

Mr. and Mrs. Walski were Anna's godparents but this was the first name day present they had given her. With trembling fingers, she opened the package and when all the paper was lifted away, she saw a small statue in blue, white and gold. It was of a woman, holding a small girl in her arms.

"Why, it's St. Anna and her little daughter, Mary," cried Mother. "That will be a keepsake for the rest of your life."

Everyone started to sing, and before long they were dancing in a circle and going in and out, first right and then left. They danced and danced, forgetting all about their work for the moment. At last, they could dance no more.

"Time for some cake," cried Mrs. Cierzan, and the ladies bustled about, cutting the cakes, making coffee and pouring milk into cups.

As Anna munched on the delicious honey cake, she thought she would explode from all the happy thoughts that were welling up inside her. She realized that she had done something unselfish, not for a minute thinking about herself, and her sisters had shared in that unselfishness. The good feeling spread through every bone and muscle in her body. She could almost feel it in her fingers and toes.

"I wish it could be like this every day," thought Anna.

The Bird Trainer

"I must get to Winona one of these days," said Father one evening late in August.

"Why not next Monday?" asked Mother. "Maybe some of the neighbors have things they need, too. We can ask on Sunday, at church."

Anna and the other children listened to Mother and Father making plans. They all wanted to go to the city, but they knew they must not ask. If they pestered and begged, like as not Father would make them all stay home.

For the rest of the week, nothing more was said about the trip. On Sunday, after Mass, Father had to attend a short meeting with the other men of the parish, so Mother joined the ladies clustered in groups at the foot of the church steps. Over and over, Anna heard Mother telling each of the groups that she would be going to the city tomorrow.

"Can I get you anything?" she asked each one.

Most of them replied that they had to go soon themselves. A few wanted her to get things they couldn't find in Dodge, in Mr. Bergaust's store. But still Mother said not a word about who would be allowed to go with her and Father.

"Maybe none of us can go," thought Anna.

That evening, Mother started packing a basket with things she would take to the city.

"Might as well leave your good dresses and stockings out, when you take them off tonight," she said to the girls. "Father says you may all come along tomorrow. Jacob and Franciszek will stay home and do the chores."

"What about me?" asked Barney.

"You can come along," answered Mother.

Barney gave a whoop of joy and the girls smiled and grinned at each other. It had been so hard to wait without saying anything, but now they were glad they had not pestered Father or Mother.

Long before it was light they were up and about. Father and Jacob curried Lord and Lady and harnessed them to the wagon. Mary and Pauline finished the milking and hurried in to wash up and change into their good clothes. Anna helped Mother make an extra big breakfast, and then they boiled eggs to take along with them for their dinner. They washed and polished a small basket of apples and put it in the wagon next to the dinner basket, under the front seat.

"Where will we sit?" asked Anna when she saw the back of the wagon. It was piled high with sacks of potatoes that Father was going to sell in Winona.

"We'll fix you a spot," said Mother. "Run and fetch me the old blanket that's in the round barrel in my room."

When Anna brought the blanket, which had been torn and mended in many spots, Mother folded it into a square and put it over the front edge of the potato sacks.

"You and Barney can perch up here. You won't fall off, will you?"

Anna shook her head, while Mother lifted her into place. Barney scrambled up next to her. Mary and Pauline sat on the wagon floor in front of the sacks, with Julian and Anton in between, and in the front seat Father held the reins while Mother held Alexander in her lap.

"All set?" asked Father.

Mother nodded and they started off.

"We're higher than everyone," Anna whispered to Barney.

"I'm the highest of all because I'm taller than you," gloated Barney.

Anna didn't mind his boasting. She was so happy to be going off to the city, she could overlook everything else.

Through the valley they drove: past the Cierzans', then the Wickas', the Tushners', the Maliszewskis' and finally out to the main road. Before long they were passing through Dodge. It was still early morning, but already there were people out in their yards, working over washtubs or splitting wood.

"We're going to the city," Anna felt like shouting to them, but of course she didn't. Even though her throne was made of potato sacks, she felt like a princess viewing her subjects.

On and on they drove. After a while Anna could feel the lumpy potatoes pressing against her thighs. With every bump in the road, they felt harder and lumpier, but Anna said not a word. She did not want to give up her high seat. At a corner halfway to Winona, Father stopped to water the horses at Mr. Carhart's farm.

"Here, have a drink." He passed a dipper first to Mother and then to each of the children. The water tasted so good, Anna could have drunk another dipperful, but Father said they must hurry on.

They were approaching Marshland when suddenly Anna spotted a group of women waiting at the side of the road. As the wagon drew closer, she saw that they were wearing leather dresses trimmed with beads. Several of the women held up woven baskets. Others were carrying bunches of reeds. Many of them had babies on their backs, bundled up in neat cradleboards.

"Indians!" whispered Barney.

Anna stared and stared. Indians had once lived in their valley but now none had homes there. Once in a while a few Indians still passed by their farm, but she rarely saw them up close.

"I wonder if one of these is the woman who brought Julian and Alexander?" she asked herself silently. But she could see only babies with dark hair and dark eyes. None were blond and light-skinned, like her two youngest brothers. "It must be another woman who brought them," thought Anna.

One of the women pointed to the potato sacks and called out something while waving her basket. It was made of woven reeds. Her dark eyes looked up at them expectantly.

"She wants to trade," said Father, and he turned to Mother with a questioning look. "Do you need another basket?"

"I guess I could use one more," answered Mother.

"And we don't want them getting angry because we won't trade."

Father held up one sack of potatoes, pointing to it and then to the basket. The woman nodded her head, and they made the exchange. Father fitted a sack of potatoes into the basket and then tucked it in as best he could, behind Anna and Barney, propping it up with other sacks on both sides.

As soon as the wagon pulled away, they started to talk excitedly about the women and the babies and how they were dressed. Anna forgot all about the bumpy, lumpy potatoes. Almost before she noticed it, they were approaching the spot on the Mississippi where the ferryboat crossed back and forth.

"Looks like we'll have to wait for a bit," said Father. "See, there's the *Turtle,* just starting to cross over to this side."

Anna shaded her eyes and followed his glance. On the far side of the river and downstream a bit, she could see a flatboat, with smoke coming out of a stack in its middle. It was slowly making its way in their direction.

"Well, it's not called the *Turtle* for nothing," said Father. "We have time for a good stretch." First he helped Mother step down, and then he swung Julian to the ground. Anton stretched out his arms. He wanted to be swung down, too.

"I hope he does it to me, too," Anna wished silently, and no sooner had she thought it than her wish came true, for Father came around to her side and held out his arms.

"Down you go!" he cried as he swooped her in a half-circle from the top of the potato sacks to the low, sandy ground.

It felt so good coming down, but it felt even better to

walk around and stretch her legs. Mother gave each of them an apple and then she went off to sit in the shade of one of the trees.

One by one, three other wagons came up to the ferry landing. Several men came on foot. They all waited for almost a half-hour before the *Turtle* came to their side of the shore. They watched as everyone on board scurried to their places. The captain called out orders and the men eased the *Turtle* into place with poles. Other men lowered a wide gangplank until it fell neatly into place, lined up with the roadway so the horses could pull the wagons off the ferry.

"All aboard!" called the captain, and when everyone who wanted to cross the river had come aboard, they raised the gangplank. Slowly, the ferry eased away from the bank, turned around in the river and headed for the opposite shore.

Father stood next to Anna by the rail.

"It will go faster in this direction," he said. "We're moving with the current."

Anna didn't want the boat to go fast. She wanted to stay on it for hours and hours.

"I wonder if this is what it feels like, crossing the Atlantic Ocean, on the way to Poland," she thought. She pretended not to see the two banks of the river, and imagined instead that there was only water, all around her, as far as she could see.

"We're almost there," said Father. "Get ready to jump back on the wagon." They all had to be in their seats when they got off the ferry, but Father would lead the horses from the front. Those were the rules.

Some of the other horses got excited and tried to rear up as they were being led off, but Lord and Lady followed

Father calmly. He paid the ferryman their fare and was just about to climb up to his seat and drive away when he noticed a crowd of people blocking Walnut Street.

"What's going on there?" he asked.

Mother stood up in front of her seat. "I can't see from here. Pull the horses closer."

Father took hold of Lady's bridle and moved the team and wagon close to the edge of the crowd.

"Why, it's a bird trainer!" cried Mother. "He has a parrot."

Anna scrambled up to the very top of the potato sacks and looked down. There, in the middle of a circle of people, stood a funny looking man, dressed in green. On his arm was perched a large bird of many colors, and behind him were several cages with other birds. In front of him was a long bench on which were painted the numbers 1 through 12.

"Oh, Frank, can't you pull the horses up and tether them to something? I'd like to watch for awhile," said Mother.

Father directed the horses off to one side of the crowd, where he saw a hitching post.

"Can you see from up there?" he asked.

"Just fine," answered Mother. "We can look over all the people's heads. Come up and see for yourself."

Father hopped up to his seat and they all stared down at the bird trainer, who now had two parrots, one on each arm. He was calling out something, and holding up the parrots, but Anna could not understand because he was speaking in English.

"What is he saying?" Mother wanted to know.

"He's calling them by their names," said Father. He could not speak English, but he had learned to under-

129

stand quite a lot when he worked in the lumber camps. "The parrot on the right is Robert and the other is Polly."

Suddenly the man set the parrots down on the bench, one at each end. He began to whistle a marching tune. Up and down marched the parrots, in time to the music, and when they met in the middle of the bench, they bowed to each other. They looked so comical that the entire crowd had to laugh.

All at once, just as the birds were bowing to each other, the trainer changed his tune to a waltz. The birds began to hop and twirl, as though they were waltzing partners.

The crowd began laughing so loudly, it was difficult to hear the whistling. But the birds kept on, dipping and bobbing and swaying. Anna was laughing so hard she had to hold on tightly to one of the potato sacks, to keep herself from falling off the wagon.

The man stopped whistling and placed a thick, wide piece of wallboard across the middle of the bench.

"Come, Robert! Open the door, Robert!"

Anna did not understand the man but soon she knew that must be what he had said, for Robert stepped up to the board, put his claw on a tiny doorknob, pushed open a small door and walked to the other side, where Polly was waiting. Again, the birds bowed to each other.

The audience clapped and Robert went through the door again.

Next, the man set a flag on the bench.

"Wave the flag, Robert. Wave the flag for our 101st Independence Day."

Robert picked up the flag and waved it back and forth. Nobody minded that Independence Day was long since gone. They all cheered lustily.

The trainer handed Robert and Polly to a boy who was helping him, and for a moment, Anna thought the show was over. Instead, the trainer opened another cage and took out a rose-colored bird with a high crest.

"Oh, what is that?" asked Anna excitedly.

"He calls it a 'cockatoo,'" answered Father, sounding out the word in English.

"Cock-a-too!" repeated Anna with a giggle. It sounded like such a funny word. Then she watched as the trainer called out something and a man stepped forward with his pocket watch. The trainer suspended the watch in front of the cockatoo for a moment, and immediately the bird stepped up to the number 10 painted on the bench, and pecked at it with his beak. Then he gave such a loud screech that everyone jumped. Even the horses gave a jerk and Anna was almost thrown off balance.

"He was telling us it's ten o'clock," explained Father. "Imagine that, a bird that can tell time!"

The trainer must have told the man with the watch to move the hands to a different hour because Anna could see him twisting the stem. Then he handed it back to the trainer. Once more it was suspended in front of the cockatoo and this time the bird ran to the number 12 and pecked at it. Again he gave a triumphant screech as the trainer held up the watch for all to see that it was set at twelve o'clock.

Now many other persons in the crowd held out their watches, each one clamoring, "Try it with my watch" or, "Here, take mine."

But the trainer did not take the watches. Instead, he pointed to a young man in the front row and asked him a question. The young man called out some numbers.

"What did he say?" asked Mother quickly.

"He asked what year he was born and the man said 1852." Father answered swiftly for he did not want to miss what would happen next.

The trainer spoke to the cockatoo: "How old is the young man?"

With a few hops, the bird first approached the number 2 and pecked at it. A few more hops and he landed at the 5 and pecked there. This was followed by his usual screeching.

"If that doesn't beat all!" Even Father was astounded. The cockatoo had correctly answered that the young man was twenty-five years old.

"How can he do that?" asked Anna.

"I don't know. He must train the bird in some special way." Father was still shaking his head in amazement and so were many other men and women in the crowd.

The trainer pointed to one more person and again the cockatoo correctly figured out the age. There was much clapping and whistling when he finished, and this time the trainer took a bow.

He tucked the rose-colored cockatoo into one of the cages, and Anna was sure that now the show would end. She looked at Father to see if he was getting ready to leave, but his eyes were still on the bird trainer.

In a moment, out stepped the young boy from behind the cages. In one hand he had Robert, and in the other was a much smaller bird, no bigger than a large sparrow. They were both dressed up in cunning little suits and on their heads were tall hats.

The trainer set both birds on the bench and then said something. Each bird picked up its hat in one claw and tipped it forward, bowing first in one direction, and then in the other.

"Oh my, oh my!" cried Father, laughing so hard he could hardly speak. "He told them they must take off their hats, because there are ladies present."

When the audience had laughed and clapped a good long while, the trainer held up his hands and put his finger to his mouth. He signaled everyone to be very quiet.

The crowd settled down and watched as the trainer brought out a copper ball and placed it on one end of the bench. Opening the ball slowly, he showed them that it was empty. Then he carefully tucked the sparrow into the ball and closed it up tight again.

Close to the other end of the bench he set down a cannon, aiming it at the copper ball. It was no bigger than a toy, but it looked like a real cannon, with a fuse string sticking out from behind.

When everything was lined up precisely, the trainer once again held his finger to his lips and an expectant hush fell over the entire crowd. Anna held her breath.

Slowly, cautiously, the trainer lit the fuse. It sizzled and sparkled.

"One, two, three!" he called out, and Robert marched up the bench to the end of the fuse.

"Fire!" cried the trainer, and Robert's right claw landed on the sizzling fuse string.

There was a loud BOOM! and a cloud of smoke surrounded the copper ball.

"Oh!" gasped everyone in the crowd. They were sure the little sparrow had been blown to bits.

Father reached for the reins to calm Lord and Lady. The noise had made them jump.

In a moment, the smoke had cleared and there, swinging on a perch sticking out from one of the cages, was the little sparrow, singing and trilling as though it were the happiest bird alive. Slowly, the trainer opened the copper ball, but—it was empty!

"How had that sparrow gotten out?" "Why hadn't the copper ball burst?" "Was the cannon shot real?" Everyone in the crowd was buzzing with questions. Now the bird trainer and his young helper were walking among the crowd, holding out their hats. Many persons tossed in bills or coins. They were pleased with the fine show. From his pocket purse, Father took out several coins. He leaned over and tossed them into the trainer's hat, as he went to untie the horses. When he stepped back up to his seat, he looked at Mother in a funny way.

"It's a foolish way to spend our hard-earned money," he said, "but it certainly was an interesting entertainment." He and Mother began to laugh and talk about the waltzing birds, and the way Robert and the sparrow had taken off their hats.

Mary and Pauline were also chattering noisily, and the boys tried to get a word in now and then but Anna was silent. She couldn't think of a thing to say. All she wanted to do was picture again the clever antics of the birds.

Through the rest of that long day, as Father and Mother went about their business, Anna thought of the birds. Through dinner and the ferry ride back over the river she thought of the birds. Through the tiring wagon ride past Marshland and Dodge and deep into their winding valley, until they came to their home, she thought of the birds. All her life she would remember them.

Diphtheria Strikes

September came, but instead of getting cooler, the weather was hotter than ever. Usually Father waited until late in the fall to harvest the corn. Sometimes he waited until early November. But this year, by early September, the corn cobs were hard and dry and the stalks had withered to a yellowy gray.

"I don't know about the other farmers in the valley, but I'm bringing in my corn now," said Father one day.

They all went to pick the cobs off the stalks. Anna and Barney and Pauline each took a row. They tore off the lower cobs and tossed them onto the wagon. Behind them came Jacob and Franciszek and Mary, who did the same with the cobs on the upper part of the stalks. They tried not to miss a single cob. Last of all came Father with his sharp hacking knife. He gave one good strong chop at the bottom of each corn plant, and then tossed the stalks into small piles that would be easy to pick up later.

Up and down the rows they went, tearing and pulling and chopping. They finished the field in one day, in time for everyone to do their other chores. As usual, Anna had to go for the sheep, which were now being pastured near the Dorawas' farm. Sometimes Barney went with her, if Father did not have much for him to do, or if he did not like the looks of the weather. They had not heard of wolves in the area for more than a year.

Czarna ziemia, kamień biały,
Czarna ziemia, kamień biały,
Siedzi na nim Podolina.

Przyszedł do niej Podoleniec,
Przyszedł do niej Podoleniec,
"Podolanko, daj mi wieniec."

Black earth, white fieldstone,
Black earth, white fieldstone,
On it sits a Podolian girl.

Up to her came a Podolian boy,
Up to her came a Podolian boy,
"Girl, give me your wreath."

Anna sang as she walked along the path toward the Dorawas'. It made her feel less alone if she sang in her loudest voice.

"Rada bym ci wieniec dała,
Rada bym ci wieniec dała,
Gdybym brata się nie bojała."

137

"Otruj, brata rodzonego,
Otruj, brata rodzonego,
Będziesz miała mnie samego."

"The wreath I would give you gladly,
The wreath I would give you gladly,
If I did not fear my brother."

"Feed your brother poison,
Feed your brother poison,
Then there will be no one in the way."

Soon she caught up with Paul Jaszewski, and they walked the rest of the way together. When they arrived at the pasture, they stared in surprise. There was Mr. Dorawa, separating out his sheep.

"Where's John?" Anna asked, but Mr. Dorawa did not seem to hear her. He herded the sheep quickly in the direction of their barn, which was not far away.

"What's the matter?" Anna asked Johnny Olszewski. Somehow, from the way Mr. Dorawa walked, she could tell something was wrong.

"They've got diphtheria at their house," blurted out Johnny. "John and Matthew and even the little baby— they're all sick."

"Diphtheria!" breathed Anna. She had heard Mother and Father talking about it last Sunday after they got home from church. Some of the children in families on the other side of Pine Creek had come down with that sickness last month. Frances Rudnik had died from it. It was a terrible thing to happen, to have diphtheria come to your house.

"Let's hope and pray it doesn't come to our valley," Mother had said, but now it had come, after all.

Silently, Paul and Anna helped Johnny herd the sheep up the incline and toward home. As soon as she had their sheep safely locked in the pen at the side of the barn, Anna hurried in to tell Mother what she had learned.

"The Dorawa children have diphtheria—all of them!" she cried.

"Merciful Heaven! Where did you get that news?" asked Mother in a shocked voice.

"Mr. Dorawa came to get their sheep. He told Johnny Olszewski about it and Johnny told us." Anna searched her mother's face fearfully. She wondered what they would do, now that diphtheria was in their valley.

"That little baby—suffering like that!" Mother shook her head and glanced over to where Alexander was sleeping. Anna knew that the little Dorawa girl had arrived only a week after her baby brother. She peeped into the cradle to look at Alexander, to make sure he was not sick, but he was sleeping peacefully and soundly.

"We'll have to make a pot of soup and send it to Mrs. Dorawa tomorrow," said Mother.

But the next day, Mrs. Jaszewski sent her daughter over with the dreadful news.

"John has taken a turn for the better, but little Matthew and the baby—they died!" She burst into tears and hurried home again.

Mother crossed herself and said a prayer. Then she turned to Anna.

"Run to Franciszek and tell him to bring me one of the cockerels. Then bring me some carrots and onions from the garden."

Soon Mother was making a delicious soup. At first, Anna pretended she couldn't smell it but the more the savory odor filled the kitchen, the hungrier she grew. She felt guilty, feeling hungry for that chicken soup, when over at the Dorawa house there was so much sorrow.

Mother put some of the soup in a smaller pot, and packed up two loaves of bread. She handed the food to Father and he tucked the pot into a corner of the wagon, carefully wrapping cloths and rags all around it. On top he put the loaves of bread.

"Ask if there's anything we can do," called Mother as he drove away.

That evening, even though it wasn't a Sunday or holiday, they ate some of the tasty chicken soup for supper. It felt strange to be eating such a special meal when they were all so sad.

"It looks as though John will recover," said Father when he came back. "He's over the worst. But the two little ones—they're gone."

"Now John will be all alone," thought Anna. "He won't have any brothers or sisters." She looked around at her own brothers and sisters. "That diphtheria had better not come over here," she thought fiercely.

All through the long, warm autumn, they watched and waited fearfully to see where the diphtheria would strike next. Even though the weather was beautiful, they did not go to church every Sunday, or visit their cousins and neighbors. Anna was not allowed to go over and play with Julia Cierzan, and Julia could not come to play with her.

Only Father went out occasionally, to Dodge, to buy or trade for the things they needed and to get the news. Almost every time, he brought the same dreadful reports: "This week the Literskis lost their youngest daughter." "Now it's by Walenski's." "I just heard that the Radomskis lost the third one yesterday."

One week in late November, when Father returned from a quick trip to Dodge, they all rushed out to meet him and find out if this time, for once, the news would be better. But Anna could see that it was not. Father was so upset he could hardly speak.

"The Felcs—they've lost their fourth one—a little girl," he told Mother, in a tight, hard voice. He looked as though he wanted to cry.

November passed into December. The unusual

weather continued, almost as warm as summer. Father plowed the fields and dug up stumps. Jacob wanted to leave for the lumber camp, but Mother would not let him go.

"We'll see. Maybe after Christmas," she said.

This year, no *gvjozdki* came their way during Advent.

"Will they come on Christmas Eve?" whispered Anna to Mother one evening after prayers. Christmas was now only a few days away.

"Hush! This is no time to be thinking about *gvjozdki*," said Mother.

Anna knew it was selfish to want her Christmas treats, when all around were families with no children left to have any Christmas at all. Yet she couldn't help feeling a little sorry for herself, and for her little brothers.

"Maybe they will come in the night, when you are asleep," said Mother, seeing her disappointment.

And that was what happened. When they returned from Midnight Mass there still was no sign of the *gvjozdki*, but on Christmas morning, next to each of their plates was a little string bag of candy. The *gvjozdki* must have been there during the night, long after they returned from church.

Mittens for a Kitten

Soon after Christmas, the warm weather finally broke. It turned sharp and cold, and a thin, powdery snow fell and covered the ground.

"Thank heavens," said Mother. "I never thought I'd be praying so much for cold weather, but it's the only thing I want right now. The colder the better. Then maybe the diphtheria will be frozen out."

All through January it stayed fiercely cold. Jacob still wanted to leave for the lumber camp, but now Father would not let him go.

"I'm thinking of making an ice house," he said, "and I need you here. If this spring and summer are as warm as last fall, we'll be glad to have some ice. Another week like this and the river should be thick enough to cut safely."

"Ice!" cried Anna. She remembered last Fourth of July in Dodge, when a man had chopped off thin wedges of ice from a big block, and gave them out to all the children who passed by. It had felt so good to suck that ice on such a hot, sunny day. Maybe Father would let them have pieces of ice next summer.

Early in February, Father went to see if the ice on the river was ready to cut. When he came back he was smiling broadly.

"Wasztok says I can cut ice by his place next week. But the best news is there hasn't been a single new diphtheria case since early January."

For the next two weeks it was bitter cold, but each day Father and Jacob and Franciszek set out on the empty bobsled. Later they came back with big, oblong chunks of ice.

"It's not as thick as I'd like," said Father, "but we can't be choosy."

He had made a lean-to shed next to the log barn, and spread a thick layer of sawdust on the ground. On top of the sawdust he and the boys lined up the chunks of ice. If there were any spaces between the chunks, they shaved or chipped off bits of ice until the blocks fit together tightly. When they had finished for the day, Father spread more sawdust over the top layer.

Anna stood and watched them, but only for a few minutes at a time. It was too cold to stand there long, in the snow outside the barn.

"Brrr! My fingers and toes are freezing," said Jacob. He stamped his feet and rubbed his hands. He and Father and Franciszek came into the house for a few minutes after they finished each load, to warm up a little.

"I need an extra pair of mittens," said Franciszek to Mother. "And another pair of stockings."

"I do, too," said Jacob.

Mother brought out two extra pairs of wool stockings but only one pair of mittens.

"This is all I have ready," she said. "We'll hurry and make another pair of mittens." But when she looked in the trunk where she kept her wool and yarn, she shook her head.

"Not enough yarn. We have to get busy spinning more wool, girls. This winter started out so warm I didn't think we'd have to spin as much as last year, but I see we're down to the last ball of yarn."

Anna liked to watch Mother or Mary or Pauline spin. They could turn the wheel just right and out would come a nice, smooth, even string of yarn. She had tried it for a few turns, but all she got were bumpy, matted lumps.

Mother began the mittens that evening, and continued working on them the next morning. By the time Father and the boys came back with the first load of ice, they were ready.

"Take them to Jacob," said Mother, handing the mittens to Anna.

Wrapping herself in her warmest shawl, Anna hurried out to the ice house. Father was at that moment starting to brush away the sawdust so he could put down the next layer of ice.

Meow! Meow! The sound of a kitten came from behind the sawdust. Suddenly, a little black head poked itself up over the edge. In its mouth was a dead mouse.

"Well, Kitty, so it's you," laughed Father. "That's fine. Keep the mice away from here. They like to make

145

their nests in sawdust, but with you around, they won't stay for long."

Anna looked at Kitty as she padded up and down the sawdust. Sometimes her paws touched the bare ice and then she would slide around.

"Her toes must be cold," thought Anna.

Kitty was not very old yet. She was one of four kittens born that fall to Mother Cat, who lived in the barn. Father had given the other kittens away, but Kitty was allowed to stay. All during the fall months she had played near the house, and every evening Anna had fed her a little milk in a tin bowl. But now Father wanted to have Kitty stay near the ice house.

"Kitty will freeze in there," Anna said to herself. Then she had a fine idea.

"I'll knit her some mittens, one for each paw."

Anna raced back to the house and went in search of her knitting needles. Mother was carding wool, and Mary was spinning.

"So you're going to help us with the knitting after all," laughed Mother. "Are you going to make a pair of mittens?"

"Yes," answered Anna, but she did not add that they would be mittens for a kitten. Last year, she had finally learned how to knit so that the rows stayed smooth and even, without puckering. Now she wanted to knit the mittens all by herself. They would be a surprise.

All that day she knitted, except for the times when she had to help wash the dishes or carry in the wood. She knitted the next day as well, stopping only for dinner and supper, and to do her chores.

"My, what a diligent little worker you are," exclaimed Mother. "But are you sure those mittens will be big enough for one of the boys? They look rather small."

"They will be just fine. You'll see." Anna smiled.

On the third day she finished the fourth mitten. They were easy to do, because she did not have to worry about fitting in a pocket for the thumb. Putting on her warm shawl, she hurried out to the ice house.

"Here, Kitty! Here, Kitty!" she called. At first Kitty did not come out from her hiding place, but Anna kept calling until at last she appeared.

"Look what I have for you," said Anna, lifting Kitty up in her arms. One by one, Anna fitted the mittens over Kitty's paws and up her legs.

Kitty did not seem to like the mittens. She pushed out her claws and they got caught in the wool. But Anna petted her and calmed her and finally slipped on the last mitten. Kitty jumped up to the top of the ice pile and looked down at Anna.

"What have you done to my legs?" she seemed to be asking, as she stretched them and tried to grasp hold of things. But she slipped and slid because her claws were now covered with wool yarn and she had no way of hanging onto the ice.

"What are you doing in here?" Father's gruff voice interrupted Anna's thought. She had not heard the bobsled coming.

Then Father glanced up at Kitty.

"What the . . ." He was speechless, but he grabbed hold of Kitty and took a good look at the mittens.

Anna smiled up at him. She was sure Father would be pleased with her surprise. But no! He frowned down at her and said in a scolding voice: "What's the idea of these contraptions? Is that the way you waste Mother's good wool? You take these off her right now and then go unravel this foolishness and knit something proper."

Anna took Kitty in her arms, and as she turned, Father gave her a spank across the bottom. She started to cry as she ran toward the house.

"Why is Father so mean?" she wondered. "I only wanted to keep Kitty warm." Struggling to keep her tears from showing, she went inside.

Mother was talking to Jacob and Franciszek and looked upset. Now she turned to Anna.

"What's the matter with you?" she asked sharply.

"I made some mittens for Kitty, to keep her warm, but Father said I have to unravel them," sobbed Anna.

"He said they were foolishness, and he spanked me."

Mother's voice softened and she took Anna to a chair. "They *are* foolishness. Kitty doesn't need mittens to stay warm. Don't you see—she has thick fur all over her. It keeps her much warmer than any mittens."

Anna looked at Kitty. It was true. She had forgotten all about Kitty's thick, spotted fur.

"But he didn't have to spank me," pouted Anna. She was still angry with her father.

"Your father's upset, Anna, because he heard some bad news today. The diphtheria hasn't gone away. It's closer than ever. A few days ago it took little Josepha Zabinski."

Anna stopped crying in an instant. Diphtheria again! And just when she had begun to think it was gone for good.

Slowly she began to extract Kitty's paws and legs from the mittens.

"I wish we could go far away from here and leave that horrible diphtheria behind," she muttered. "I wish we could go to Poland."

Mother shook her head sadly.

"Now you *are* talking foolishness," she said. "In Poland we had something even more dreadful than diphtheria. That was one of the reasons your father and I left—to get away from the cholera."

Anna did not ask what cholera was. She didn't want to hear anything more about it, or about diphtheria, either. She just wished they could go someplace where they would be safe from all sickness.

"We have to hope and pray that it comes to an end soon," said Mother.

Ice for the Apple Trees

Lent began in late February, and with it, the warm weather returned. By the first week in March, the tips of all the tree branches and twigs were covered with buds of pale green.

"If this weather keeps up, the apple trees will bloom," said Father. "I don't like it at all. There's sure to be a hard frost later and then we won't get any fruit."

The next day was warmer than ever.

"Isn't there something we can do?" asked Mother.

"I'll try," replied Father. "Good thing we put in the ice."

He went to the ice house and brushed away the sawdust from one of the chunks. Then he pushed the ice block into a wheelbarrow, together with his hatchet and a pick, and a pile of gunnysacks. Anna followed behind to see what Father would do next.

As soon as he came to the cluster of fruit trees, he began to chop the ice into smaller slabs. He propped four slabs up close to an apple tree, near the roots, and then wound the gunnysacks around the ice to hold it in place. He did the same to each of the other six apple trees, working fast so the ice would not melt too quickly.

"You keep an eye on them," said Father to Anna. "Come and tell me when the ice is all melted."

At first, Anna stayed right by the trees, watching carefully to see whether the ice had melted completely away. But then she realized that the ice would last a few hours, wrapped up as it was in the gunnysacks. So she ran to help Mother in the garden, and went to check on the ice only every now and then.

Mother sprinkled holy water on some of the vegetable seeds.

"It won't hurt if we plant a few now," she said. "Should the frost come again, we'll still have plenty of seeds left." With extreme care, she seeded a short row each of carrots, kohlrabi and lettuce, using only as many seeds as were absolutely necessary.

By the time they had finished dinner, the ice around the trees had all melted. Once again Father hauled more chunks from the ice house and wrapped them tightly around the tree trunks.

"Twice a day ought to do it," he said. "It's cold enough at night to keep the sap from rising."

All through March Father hauled ice out to the fruit trees. The pile inside the ice house began to get smaller and smaller.

"I hope there's some left for summer," thought Anna.

Mother's plants came up and grew bigger and bigger. By the end of March they were eating the first lettuce, and the kohlrabi heads began to form. The meadows all around were thick with grass.

The trees at the side of the house and all through the woods were completely covered with green leaves. Only the seven fruit trees were still mostly bare. Here and there a clump of blossoms had burst through at the end of a branch. It looked as though someone had flung a few bouquets into the bare branches, to make them seem less out of place in the green world surrounding them.

"How long can you keep it up?" asked Mother, as Father prepared to go once more to prop ice around the trees.

"The ice should last until Easter," answered Father. "By then, it will be safe to stop."

"Mercy on us!" cried Mother. "Easter isn't until late in April. I hope we get the last frost before then." She didn't say it, but Anna knew that Mother was thinking more about diphtheria than about apple trees. Over on the Wicka farm, just down the valley road a little, all the children were sick, and two had already died.

Now, when Father came back with more news of diphtheria, he didn't say out loud what he had heard. He waited until he could speak quietly to Mother, and then he would tell only her.

One evening, Anna crept out of bed to get a drink of water. Through a crack in the curtain she saw that the lamp was still lit in the kitchen. She had been ready to push aside the curtain when she heard her parents talking, and held back.

"I still think I should go and offer to lend Mary Wicka a hand, Frank."

"No! It's best you stay here." Father's voice was firm. "You heard what Father Snigourski said. We should keep to home as much as possible. Besides, Pete Zywitski told me his wife was helping to take care of things."

"Oh, Frank, I feel so helpless. What if it should hit here next?" wailed Mother, and she burst into sobs.

"Hush! Don't talk about it. Nothing's going to happen," said Father, trying to comfort her.

Anna knew she shouldn't be listening. She crept back into bed, forgetting about her drink of water. From the kitchen came the sound of low, murmuring voices, first Father's, then Mother's. For a long time, Anna could not fall asleep, thinking of the Wicka children and her mother's sobbing.

A few days later came the worst news of all. Two more of the Wicka children had died. Mary whispered it to Anna when she came in from rounding up the sheep late one afternoon, and found Mother openly weeping as she prepared supper. Too young to understand, Julian and Alexander sat quietly in a corner, staring at Mother and wondering why she was acting so strangely.

The days of April crept slowly by. Father and Mother hardly spoke, and the children tried to be as quiet as possible, as though they were afraid to draw attention to themselves. Anna prayed to her guardian angel every day.

"Please, please keep the diphtheria from coming here."

On Thursday of Holy Week, she awoke very early, with a strange feeling. Poking her head out from under the blankets, she realized it was colder than usual. Out of bed she hopped, and still in her flannel nightgown, she ran into the kitchen. Mother was humming a tune as she prepared their breakfast.

Anna scurried to the window, but she could see nothing at all. A thick lace of frost covered the panes. She ran to the door, opened it, and stood stock-still, staring straight ahead.

Everything was covered with a thick white frost that sparkled and glistened in the sunshine. Every branch of every tree, every leaf and twig on every branch, every blade of grass and every single thing that stood in the yard was coated with the shining frost.

"Oh!" breathed Anna. "Everything has a mitten of white."

"Close the door, Anna. And get dressed." Mother's voice did not sound cross or scolding. And she still did not seem upset when they later walked to the garden and saw the lettuce and other plants wilting under the layer of frost.

"We might as well pick all the lettuce and kohlrabi," said Mother. "It won't be good after today. Never mind. We can plant more."

For dinner and supper they ate raw, crispy chunks of kohlrabi and mounds of lettuce with sweet cream dressing.

On Good Friday, during the night, it snowed enough to cover the ground, and during most of Holy Saturday the snow continued to come down.

"If this isn't a topsy-turvy year!" exclaimed Father. "We had to take the wagon to church on Christmas Eve because there was no snow, and now, if we want to go to church for Easter, we'll have to get out the bobsled!"

"Oh, Frank, do you think we should?" asked Mother fearfully.

"I'm church secretary. You know I have to be there," said Father. "But I shouldn't think there's any harm now if you go with the children as well. We'll hurry back. Yes, by golly, I think we *will* all go. I'll get the bobsled cleaned up and ready."

Anna didn't want to go at first but as the day wore on and the snow grew deeper, she thought how much fun it would be, gliding along in the sled. When Mother took the special Easter bread out of the oven, everything smelled so crisp and fresh and new that she was sure it was all right to go out now.

"That diphtheria is miles away by now," she thought as she tumbled into bed. "I'm sure it went off in the other direction, just like the wolves."

Easter

On Easter morning Mother woke Father very early, without saying a word. Anna dressed quickly and wrapped her shawl around her shoulders. As soon as she was ready, Mother handed her two empty pails and a dipper, still without speaking.

Anna knew that on Easter morning they must first take a drink of the newly blessed spring water, before they spoke to each other.

"Why do we do that?" she had once asked.

"Water means life," answered Mother. "Easter is our start of new life each year, so we drink fresh spring water to remind us of that."

Luckily, the spring was not far away. Anna trudged

through the light snow which crackled under her feet almost like dried leaves. The sun was coming over the hill behind Glenzinski's farm, putting a sparkly shine on everything.

She broke through the thin layer of ice that covered the path of the spring water. Taking the dipper, she held it below the narrow stream of water trickling down, and when it was full she emptied it into one of the pails. There was no room to fit the pail under the trickle, so Anna had to fill the dipper again and again before she had enough water in each pail. Carrying the pails carefully so as not to spill them, she hurried home.

When they sat down to eat breakfast, Father blessed the new spring water with a prayer. Then he lowered the dipper into one of the pails, brought it up full of water, and took a sip. After that, he passed the dipper to each of the children so they could take a drink before they ate anything. Mother and Father and Jacob ate nothing at all, because they were going to receive Holy Communion. Instead, while the children ate, Mother poured some of the spring water into two bottles. These she placed in the corner of a large basket, next to a cloth full of colored eggs. On top of the eggs, with a cloth in between, she put the Easter bread.

Anna had tried to peek at the eggs before they were put into the basket, but Mother had quickly spread the cloth over all the cracks.

"You'll see them when we get back from church," she said.

The service that morning was long. First, Father Snigourski blessed the water he would use for baptisms during the coming year. While he did that, everyone held up bottles and containers of water, so they would be blessed, too. Then he said many other prayers before he finally started the Mass. During the Offertory, Mother and Father held up the basket of bread and eggs to be blessed.

After Mass, they waited for a few minutes while Father arranged his parish business with the men, and Mother talked to the women she had not seen since the beginning of Lent. They wept a bit and shook their heads in sorrow over the recent deaths.

"I hope we've heard the last of the bad news about diphtheria," said Mother nervously.

"Yes, pray God it's the end," agreed Mrs. Walski.

Father and the men hurried to finish their discussion and then he rounded up the family. "Quickly now. Jump on the sled. This snow will thaw before noon." He urged the horses home as fast as they could trot.

Once more they sat down to eat, but first Father took one of the eggs out of the basket and peeled away the golden brown shell. He salted it, took a small bite, and passed it on to Mother. After she had a bite, Jacob took his turn, then Franciszek, and on around the table, until there was only a tiny bit left for Alexander. When the egg was finished, they ate the delicious Easter bread, and smoked sausages that Mother had saved.

"Now I'll divide the eggs," said Mother, reaching for the basket. She unfolded the cloth and they could see pale, rose-colored eggs that had got their color from berry juice; golden yellow eggs that had been boiled with onion skins; deep blue eggs that had soaked in elderberry juice for hours; and eggs of purplish red that had stood in beet juice for a few days.

"What a lot of eggs!" exclaimed Anna. Though they used eggs in cooking, eggs alone they had only for special meals.

"It's taken me weeks to save them," said Mother. "And this will be all we can eat for some time. I must save all the layings from the next few weeks for hatching out." She put first one egg in front of each plate, then a second, a third and a fourth.

One of the eggs by Barney's plate began to roll to the edge of the table.

"Catch it! It's falling!" cried Anna, but the egg landed on the floor and the pretty pink shell cracked in many places.

"Oh, well, I guess that means I can eat it right away," said Barney.

"You let it roll on purpose," Anna accused him.

"No, I didn't."

"Yes, you did."

"Quarreling on Easter morning?" asked Mother. "Shame on you both! Go on and eat it, Barney, but that will be all for today. You must save some for *Dyngus*."

"What is *Dyngus?*" asked Julian.

"Don't you remember? It is a custom we brought from the Old Country," explained Mother. "On Easter Monday, the boys sprinkle the girls with water and give them a switching until the girls agree to give up their eggs."

Anna looked at her eggs. They were all such pretty colors.

"Which should I eat today?" she asked herself. "I know. The rose-colored one. Then Barney can't get a second one from me tomorrow."

The next day, Anna knew she would have to plan carefully if she did not wish to give up all her eggs. She ran out to get water very early while the boys were still doing their chores. Poor Mary and Pauline! They were both caught on the way back from milking, and each had to give an egg to Jacob, Franciszek and Barney. Now the two girls had no eggs left.

"We'll get you, too," laughed Jacob as he pointed at Anna. "Just wait and see."

Anna did not go outside unless she had to, and always looked carefully in all directions before she closed the door. By mid-afternoon, she still had her eggs.

"Anna," called Mother. "Aren't you forgetting something? There's hardly any wood left by the stove."

Anna hadn't forgotten. She was waiting for the boys to go out first, off to the barn. Then she would hurry and bring in the wood as fast as she could.

She looked at Jacob and Franciszek, hoping for a sign that they would soon be on their way. As if he had heard her secret wish, Jacob stood up and stretched.

"Time to do the chores," he said.

Franciszek and Barney got up, too, and followed him without a word.

Anna waited for ten minutes before she put on her knitted wool jacket and scarf. It had warmed up enough so she did not need her shawl. She opened the door, peered out to see that no one was waiting, and ran toward the woodpile.

No sooner had she reached it than three loud voices howled triumphantly. Jacob, Franciszek and Barney appeared and quickly surrounded her, brandishing their willow switches and small bottles of water.

"Now we've got you cornered," crowed Barney, and then the three brothers chanted in unison:

Dyngus, Dyngus, po dwa jaja!
Nie chcę chleba tylko jaja!

Dyngus, Dyngus, for two eggs!
Don't give me bread, only eggs!

They sprinkled Anna with water and lightly spanked her on her backside with the willow switches.

"All right," sighed Anna. "I'll get my eggs." Now she wouldn't have any left either.

"Don't be sad," said Mother. "You can get them back tomorrow. When I was little, I was always glad that the girls played *Dyngus* after the boys, because then they couldn't take the eggs away again."

The next morning Anna, Pauline and Mary got up very early. They played the same trick on their brothers, waiting for them behind the barn. Before they had even started milking, they each had their eggs back again.

"There are a lot of boys at the Olszewski house," said Mother in an offhanded voice as they were finishing breakfast. "I shouldn't wonder if they still have most of their eggs."

Anna looked at Pauline and Pauline looked at Mary.

"Mother, may we pay a visit to Aunt Bridget this morning?" asked Mary sweetly.

"I think that's a fine idea," answered Mother. "I'll send along some of my Easter bread." She wrapped a loaf in a white cloth and handed it to Mary.

The girls took their willow switches and a bottle of water and walked in the direction of the Olszewski homestead. The weather had turned so warm again that the snow was melting fast. All along the path, tiny blue crocuses were pushing their heads through the last patches of snow.

When they drew near the barn, they could see Joe and Johnny Olszewski, and their stepbrothers Frank and Nicholas, carrying pails of water toward the barn. Their backs were to the three girls.

"Let's stand outside the door and wait for them to come out," suggested Pauline.

Quickly and quietly, they ran to the side of the barn and then sidled up to the doorway, readying their willow switches. Pauline held the bottle of water, preparing to sprinkle the boys as soon as they appeared in the doorway. Mary clutched the Easter bread in her left arm.

From the inside of the barn, they could hear the soft murmur of the boys' voices and the splash of water being poured into drinking troughs. Then, the voices got louder.

"That should be enough water for the day," Joe was saying as he came out the door, followed by John, Frank and Nicholas.

Dyngus, Dyngus, po dwa jaja!
Nie chcę chleba tylko jaja!

Dyngus, Dyngus, for two eggs!
Don't give me bread, only eggs!

Laughing and shrieking, the girls leaped out from behind the door, flailing their switches at the four boys. Pauline danced around them, sprinkling the water in all directions so that some would fall on each of them. She sprinkled until the bottle was empty.

"Watch out!"

"Run for the house!"

"You sneaky cousins!"

"It's not fair!" yelled the boys, as they tried to dodge out of the way. "We didn't come to you for *Dyngus!*"

"No one stopped you," said Anna saucily. "Now give us some eggs."

"That won't leave any for us," complained Johnny.

"Too bad," said Pauline in a mock serious voice. "Sisters, shall we take only one egg from each, so our poor cousins won't cry?"

While Pauline was speaking, Anna noticed the barn door swinging open. Suddenly, out darted their cousin Paul, coming up behind Mary.

"You won't be giving me a sprinkle," he shouted, giving her left arm a push. He did not see that she was carrying the cloth-wrapped bread, but thought she had a water bottle.

Into the air sailed the parcel of bread. It landed with a plop, in the melting snow and mud of the barnyard. The white cloth spread open and the round loaf rolled into a patch of snow.

Anna gasped and so did her sisters and cousins. They

had been taught that it was sinful to mishandle bread.

Mary darted over to the loaf, picked it up, brushed off the snow, and kissed it, whispering a little prayer. She held it out to the other children, and they each kissed it in turn.

"It didn't get dirty," said Anna hopefully.

"No, it landed in the snow," added Paul encouragingly. He was too embarrassed to apologize.

The white cloth was too muddy and wet to wrap around the bread again. Sheepishly, Mary carried the loaf into the house and handed it to Aunt Bridget. Pauline held the dirty cloth by one corner. Anna and the boys stood behind her.

"It fell in the mud," said Mary, blushing a little.

Aunt Bridget looked the loaf over carefully. Then she smiled.

"Did you girls come over for *Dyngus?*" she asked.

"Yes," answered Anna quickly. "And we caught the boys. Now they have to give us eggs."

"It's a good thing you caught them early in the day," said Aunt Bridget. "I don't think they have but one egg left—maybe two."

Joe and Johnny and Frank and Nicholas each handed over one egg, but Paul put both of his remaining eggs in Mary's hands. He didn't say anything, but Anna could see he was grateful that they hadn't told Aunt Bridget it was he who had knocked the bread down.

"Now I have five eggs," gloated Anna as the girls were walking home. "One for each day until Sunday."

The Tramps

"Midsummer Day, start to make hay," chanted Father on the morning of June 20. "It's a good thing the weather has cleared up a bit."

All day he swished with his scythe at the hay on the hillside, while Jacob and Franciszek cut the hay on the level parts of the field. But once the hay was cut, the sticky, humid weather returned. Every evening it would rain a little, and the days were overcast and moist.

Father and the boys turned the hay over several times, but it was still not dry enough to gather up.

"At this rate it's going to rot on the fields," complained Father. He went about with a worried look, until at last, one afternoon, it cleared up. There was no rain that evening, and the next day dawned bright and sunshiny. As soon as the dew had been burned off by the sun, Father went out to turn the hay one last time.

That same morning, Mary, Julian and Alexander woke up feeling sick. At first, Mother was frightened, thinking the diphtheria had come back. She tried to get them to eat some breakfast, but they each vomited the food back up. Then she felt their foreheads; they were not hot or damp with fever.

"Does your throat feel sore?" she asked Julian. He shook his head.

"It must be the summer complaint," said Mother. She sent them back to bed and all morning checked up on them every few minutes, carefully watching for signs of further illness.

"It's not diphtheria, Mother," said Mary weakly, from her bed. "I'll be fine in a day or two. It's just in my stomach."

When Father came in for dinner he was smiling broadly.

"If we all work at it this afternoon," he said as he sat down at the table, "we should be able to get the hay in."

"I can't leave Mary and the little boys here alone," argued Mother. "Not the way they are feeling."

Mary was not at the dinner table. She was lying down in her bed and still wanted nothing to eat. Julian and Alexander were also missing from their places on the bench. They were asleep in Mother's bed.

Father said nothing. He wanted very much to get in all the cut hay, but he knew they could not manage it without Mother's help. She was so quick and handy at tying up the bundles with twisted strands of hay that were almost as strong as ropes.

"I could stay and watch them," offered Anna. "They'll probably sleep most of the afternoon anyway."

Father looked at Mother with a question in his eyes.

"I suppose that would be all right." Mother's voice didn't sound completely convinced. "You would have to come and get me if they took a turn for the worse."

"I would," promised Anna.

"Then I guess I can go, at least until it's time for you to get the sheep," said Mother.

Father breathed a sigh of relief. They quickly finished their dinner and set off for the hay field, leaving Anna with the dishes.

Humming to herself the whole time, she washed and dried the tin cups and plates and tidied up the kitchen. Then, taking a broom, she swept the floor. After that, she sat down in the rocker, thinking of what she must do next. It was so quiet in the house, she could hear every little noise. It was rather scary, being there alone.

From the bedroom came the sound of one of the boys, whimpering, and Anna jumped up.

"I'm not alone," she told herself. "Mary and Julian and Alexander are here." She went in to have a look at the boys. Mother had said she should try to get them to take sips of spring water.

Julian was awake. He looked up at her listlessly.

"Do you want a drink?" whispered Anna, so as not to wake Alexander. Julian sat up and nodded his head.

Anna returned to the kitchen and reached for the dipper in the water bucket. There was only a little water left. She tipped the bucket to the side, scooped up half a dipperful and took it in to Julian. He drank one small sip and pushed the dipper aside. Then he flopped back onto his pillow and closed his eyes. He wanted to sleep again.

Anna tiptoed back into the kitchen.

"I might as well go now to get more water from the spring," she told herself. Picking up the bucket, she went to the door, opened it, and stepped outside.

The moment she did, she dropped the bucket, gave a little jump and then stood stock-still. Standing in front of her, just a few feet away, were two strange men. They were dressed in raggedy clothes and had dark, bushy beards and uncombed hair.

"Hello, little girl," one of them called out in English.

Anna turned, opened the door, leaped into the house and slammed the door shut. Into their bedroom she ran, and shook Mary awake.

"Mary, get up! Two strange men . . . at the door." Anna was so breathless with fear and excitement she could hardly bring out the words.

Mary looked at her with bewildered eyes.

"Two funny looking men are at the door," repeated Anna.

Without a word, Mary got up and went into the kitchen. As she moved toward the door, the two girls heard a loud knocking. They looked at each other fearfully.

"Shall we open it?" asked Mary.

"Better not," whispered Anna.

The knocking sounded at the door again, louder than before.

"They might break the door down," said Mary as she moved closer to it.

"Don't open it," pleaded Anna. But Mary had already taken the knob and opened the door a crack.

"What do you want?" she asked the men in Polish.

"No speak Polish," one of the men replied. "English."

Mary struggled to remember the few English words she had learned in school.

"You . . . hungry?" she asked.

Both men nodded their heads vigorously, and started saying something.

Mary turned her head back to Anna: "We'd better fix them a plate of something to eat. Maybe then they'll go away. Is there anything left from dinner?"

"Some boiled potatoes Mother wanted to fry up for supper."

"Put them on two plates, with a chunk of bread for each. Hurry!"

While Anna ran to get out two of the tin plates, Mary turned to the men again.

"One minute . . . food," she said. They eyed her up and down, but did not move.

Anna dumped the potatoes in two heaps onto the tin plates. She took two fat slices of bread left from dinner, smeared them with lard and sprinkled them with salt. Balancing the plates, one in each hand, she walked to the door. Mary opened it wide enough for her to pass through and she marched up to the two men, trying not to show how much she was trembling inside.

She thrust the plates into their hands and scurried back into the house.

"Forks! I forgot forks!" she gasped. She hated the thought of having to go out to the men again.

"They'll eat with their fingers," Mary assured her after she had shut the door tight.

The two girls looked out the window. Through the wavery glass they could see the men walking swiftly toward the woodpile. Almost before they sat down on some stumps there, they were gobbling up the food, pushing it into their mouths with their fingers.

"Do you think they'll go away when they finish eating?" asked Anna anxiously.

"I hope so," sighed Mary. She felt weak and useless. "I have to sit down for awhile," she said, collapsing into the rocking chair.

Anna kept staring out the window.

"They've finished," she announced, as she saw the

men put the tin plates down on the stumps and get up.

"They're going away," she cried excitedly as the men moved off toward the road.

"Oh, no! They're not!" The men had turned and were now walking in the direction of the barn. They peered inside and then walked around behind it.

"I can't see them! What could they be doing behind the barn?" wailed Anna.

At that moment the men appeared around the corner again and began to walk once more in the direction of the house.

"They're coming to the house again!" shrieked Anna.

Mary breathed a prayer aloud, and Anna joined in. They continued praying until, once again, there was a knocking on the door.

"Don't open it," pleaded Anna.

"I must," answered Mary. "They might get angry and knock it down. If we're polite and friendly to them, maybe they'll go away." She got up, went to the door, and slowly opened it.

Now only one of the men started speaking, as he handed back the tin plates. Mary could make out the word "Thanks," so she felt more confident now that the men would go away. But then she heard what he said after that, and made out the words "Father" and "money."

"Oh, Mother of God, my dear sweet patron, help us," moaned Mary under her breath.

"What did he say?" whispered Anna.

"I think he's asking where Father keeps his purse of money," answered Mary.

"*We* don't even know where Father keeps it," Anna protested.

"I know. But will they believe us? We've got to do something." Mary stood thinking for a moment. Then she poked her head out the door, said "Please" and closed it again.

"Mother has some of that dried beef left, doesn't she?" asked Mary.

"Yes. The two chunks she always saves for the Fourth of July—they're hanging up in a corner of the attic."

"Bring them down to me," ordered Mary. "Maybe if we offer them such a treat, they'll go away."

Anna climbed swiftly up the ladder. With two strong jerks she tore the long thick strips of dried beef from their hooks and then went to the ladder opening.

"Here, catch," she called to Mary and tossed them down. By the time she had climbed down the ladder, Mary was slicing the dried beef in thick slices. She was too nervous to make them thin and slivery, the way Mother did. The deep, smoky smell of the beef spread through the kitchen, making Anna's mouth water. After Mary had finished cutting she scooped up the slices in her hands.

"Open the door," she ordered again.

Anna opened it and Mary took the sliced beef out to the men, thrusting it into their hands.

"Now, go!" she commanded, motioning to the road.

The men simply stared at her, so she went back into the house and closed the door again.

Both Anna and Mary went to the window and peeped out.

"Oh, no!" moaned Mary. "They're sitting by the woodpile again."

The two men sat there, chewing and chewing on the tasty dried beef. The girls watched them silently for at least five minutes.

172

"You'll have to go to the hay field to get Father," said Mary finally.

"What if they try to grab hold of me as I go past the woodpile?" asked Anna in a scared voice.

"You mustn't go that way. I'll let you out the back window and then you must run down below, along the lower side of the hill, so they can't see you. Come. You'd better start right now."

They went to their back bedroom and opened the window as quickly as they could. Anna had to push up hard, because Mary had hardly any strength. Then she climbed on a chair, let herself up onto the sill and looked back at Mary before she dropped to the ground.

"What will you do while I'm gone?" asked Anna in a whisper.

"Don't worry. I'll be all right. I'll find something to put in front of the door. Just run as fast as you can."

Anna jumped down, ran almost to the bottom of the hill, then turned to follow the path around the lower edge. Fearfully she glanced up toward the top, to see if the men had heard her and were looking down, but she could see no sign of them.

All along the edge of the hill she sped, following the cow path as best she could. When she knew she had passed far beyond the woodpile, she began to climb upward, so that she could eventually cross over in back of the barn and go to the hay field.

The hill was steep and rocky and sometimes she slid back as many steps as she climbed forward. She clutched at small clumps of weeds or bushes, pulling herself up the steepest parts. All the while she was running or climbing, she kept thinking about Father and how annoyed he would be at having to come in from the hay field. But then she would think of poor Mary, fighting off the two men all alone, and she would try to go faster.

At last she reached the level field behind the barn, where she could run faster. Now she felt a pain in her side, like a stitch pulling at her insides. She could hardly move without doubling up. Her breath came in gasps.

"I must go on," she thought. "I must go on."

Suddenly, up ahead, climbing to the crown of the hay field, she saw the loaded wagon, with Father directing the team skillfully from the side. Anton, Barney and Pauline were laughing as they jounced and bounced on the top. Father noticed Anna now and brought the horses to a stop.

"Whoa! What's the matter?" he called out.

"Two strange men . . . house . . . won't go away!" Anna called as best she could, taking big gulps of air and trying to catch her breath.

Father tossed the reins to Franciszek and called out:

"Bring them in." Already, he was running toward the house as fast as he could. Mother followed, moving her legs forward as quickly as her skirts would allow. Anna ran at her side.

"Those men. Did they do anything to you?" Mother choked out the words as she ran.

Anna shook her head. She was too out of breath to explain any more. Up ahead, she could see Father pause in the yard long enough to give one quick look around. Then he continued loping toward the house. He was still trying to push open the door when Mother and Anna came rushing up.

"I can't get the door open!" cried Father. He had a wild look in his eyes.

"Mary! Marysia!" called Mother.

In answer, they heard a soft moan.

"The window!" shouted Anna. "I came through the window in back."

They raced to the back of the house, and there was the window still wide open. Father leaped up to the sill and wriggled inside. Mother tried to lift herself up, but the sill was too high off the ground.

"Boost me up," begged Anna. She wanted to go and help Father.

"No," answered Mother sharply. "We won't go in until we know it's safe."

They waited for only a minute but it seemed an eternity. Mother could bear it no longer.

"Frank!" she called loudly through the window. "Frank! What are you doing?"

At last, Father appeared at the window.

"It's all right," he said. "It's all right. Come around to the door and I'll let you in."

Back they ran to the front of the house, and now the

door opened slowly, but only part way. Mother squeezed in, and Anna followed her. She gulped in fright and astonishment at what she saw. There, on the floor, leaning a bit against the side wall, lay Mary. Her eyelids were fluttering and her face was so white it looked as though it were made of china, like Mother's name day plate. In front of the door, and now pushed slightly forward, was the big, wooden kitchen cupboard.

In an instant, Mother was down on the floor.

"Mary, my Marysia," she whispered. "What's the matter? Did the men hurt you?"

Mary shook her head. "The cupboard . . . I pushed it . . . door . . . then I don't remember."

"She must have fainted," said Mother, glancing up at Father with an agonized look. "Do you think. . . ?"

"Hush!" warned Father. "I'm sure nothing happened. The cupboard was right up against the door. I don't think they got in."

"But the window . . ."

"I don't think they even went around to the back," Father reassured her. "Tell me, Anna, where were they when you came to get us?"

Then Anna told them all about the men: how they had appeared so suddenly, and how raggedy and dirty they had looked; how she and Mary had fed them potatoes and bread, and then, when they didn't go away, how they had brought out the dried beef, in hopes that that would satisfy them.

"When I left, they were sitting near the woodpile, chewing the dried beef. Mary told me I had to run down to the path below the hill so they wouldn't see me. So I did," Anna finished her story.

"Like as not they heard the wagon coming back and

got scared off," said Father. "The least they could have done was stay around to lend a hand."

Mother helped Mary stand up and then she gently eased her into the rocking chair.

"They said something about Father and his money," whispered Mary. "But I couldn't understand. I thought they were meaning to rob us." Tears began to roll down her cheeks.

"Now don't get upset," Father calmed her. "They were probably only asking if I'd pay money for work. A lot of the neighbors have told me they're being pestered by tramps these days, looking for jobs. I'm sure these two weren't looking for trouble. But you did the right thing by sending Anna for us."

"I can tell you, I'm not leaving my girls in the house alone any more, hay or no hay," insisted Mother.

"I think you're right," agreed Father. "No amount of hay is worth harm coming to our girls. We'll bring in as much as we can this afternoon and hope for the best. But one thing is for sure—we're getting a dog to warn us when strangers come."

Fourth of July

"Aren't you glad we have Guardian to stay behind and watch the farm?" exclaimed Anna as their wagon started off on the road to Dodge.

True to his word, Father had bought their new watchdog less than a week after the tramps had visited the farm. Now he had to stay behind while they went off to enjoy the festivities.

Anna felt sorry for Guardian. She was about to call out: "I'll save you a slice of dried beef." Then she remembered they had none left this year. But there was cold fried chicken and boiled eggs and *pączki*. They would still have a feast.

"I hope they have ice, like last year," said Anna.

Father had no ice left at all, but maybe someone in Dodge had a bigger ice house.

Once again they lined up for the annual parade. Each time they passed the leafy decorations lining the street, Anna thought they were prettier.

"I'll never get tired of Fourth of July parades," she sighed with contentment.

"You would, if you had them every day," said Mother.

Anna didn't think so.

Then it was time to settle down for the speeches. Father drove their wagon up to a free spot, next to Aunt Bridget and the rest of the Olszewski family. On the other side of them were Mr. and Mrs. Konkel and their children and grandchildren. The Konkels had come from Poland at the same time as Mother and Father and lived in another valley, on the other side of Pine Creek.

As soon as the speeches were over, everyone ate dinner. After they had finished, Father stood up and looked around for some card playing partners. No sooner had he started to move off in the direction of the school than a big BOOM! echoed through Dodge.

"There goes that Charlie Kassimor again," laughed Father.

Once again, the children and young people sauntered over to the blacksmith shop, to watch the anvils being fired. Four times Mr. Kassimor made the anvil leap into the air as though it weighed no more than a pine cone. And each time the audience held their ears to block out the sound.

"Honestly, I don't know why we come so close to watch," complained Mary with a laugh. "All it does is make our ears hurt."

"But it's exciting," argued Anna.

When the anvil firing was over, the girls walked back to the wagon, where Mother sat chatting with Mrs. Konkel and Aunt Bridget.

"Why don't you start a little dancing," suggested Mother. "We'll sing along so you have the music." She started a song and the other ladies joined in:

Jeszcze zespól dalej, jeszcze żywo dalej,
Jeszcze żywo dalej, na lewo.
Jeszcze zespól dalej, jeszcze żywo dalej,
Jeszcze żywo dalej, na prawo.

Now the group goes forward, now go quickly
    forward,
Now go quickly forward to the left.
Now the group goes forward, now go quickly
    forward,
Now go quickly forward to the right.

Mary and Anna joined hands, beginning to move to the sound of the music. Then Pauline and several of the other girls standing around stepped in and formed a circle. Around and around they went, following the words of the song. More women joined in the group of singers surrounding them.

Two little girls stood off to the side, watching the dancing wistfully. Anna didn't know who they were but she had heard them speaking English.

"They don't have to know Polish to dance with us," she thought, and she waved them to come into the circle.

Eagerly the girls joined in. They tried their best to follow the steps but it seemed as though they *would* have to understand Polish to do the dance, because they never knew when to turn right or left. They would follow the steps correctly for a while and then bump! Because they turned at the wrong moment in the wrong direction, they collided with the dancers next to them. Then everyone would tumble down in a heap, giggling and laughing. Quickly they would get up and start over again.

Anna didn't mind their mistakes. She thought it was fun dancing with the English-speaking girls, because of the unexpected way they did things. But Mary wanted them to dance properly.

"Left! Now right! Down the middle!" She called out the directions in English the next time they started a dance.

All went well for a while until Mary forgot and called "Left" when she really meant "Right."

Smack! One of the girls waved her arms in the wrong direction and hit Anna hard on the back. Down she went, on her stomach, with the girl on top of her. The rest of the group was in a shambles.

Mother and the other ladies were laughing so hard they couldn't sing.

"That will have to be all," she gasped. "I can't sing when you are constantly making me laugh."

The two English-speaking girls now motioned to Anna and the other Polish-speaking girls to form a line. They clasped their hands and held them high and arching, like a bridge. Then they began to sing a song.

"They want us to go under," said Mary, so she started the line moving. In and out they went, ducking under the bridge of hands. Suddenly, the two girls lowered their arms and caught Anna.

"It's like Father, with the trap for the hare," thought Anna, so she tried to wiggle free. But the girls motioned for her to wait a moment. They sang a bit longer while they swayed back and forth with her still caught between their arms and then she had to stand off to the side, behind one of the girls.

Over and over again the line passed through until all the girls had been captured between the falling arms, and then separated into one of the two lines behind the English-speaking girls. Then the two lines had a tug of war until one line tumbled down.

All afternoon the girls played and danced and sang, sometimes in Polish and sometimes in English. Finally, Anna flopped down on the grass near Mother, tired and out of breath.

"I can't make another move," she said.

"Not even for some ice cream?" asked Mother.

"Ice?" asked Anna, because that's what she thought she had heard.

"No. Ice cream," repeated Mother. "Mrs. Bergaust has made some and they're beginning to serve it now. We must take some plates and cups. Pauline, you run and fetch Father. He'll want his share."

Quickly Anna picked up a tin cup and a spoon and walked to the front of Bergaust's store. Many boys and young men were standing around, watching.

"Look!" cried Barney. "They finished turning it."

He stepped aside and Anna saw a big tub filled with ice; in the middle of the ice was a large pail of something that looked cold and creamy. Mother paid Mrs. Bergaust and then she was allowed to dip her big spoon ten times into the ice cream, scooping it into the plates and cups they had brought.

"Now we must hurry back to eat it before it melts," said Mother.

Never had Anna tasted anything better than the cold, velvety ice cream of that afternoon. It tingled on her

182

tongue as it melted and then slid down her throat. It was much, much better than sucking on plain ice.

No one spoke as they took turns eating the ice cream. They had to share the spoons because Mother had brought only three. Each of the children got five or six small bites and then the ice cream was gone.

"I wish I could lick the bottom of the cup," thought Anna. She wanted to get out every drop of the delicious ice cream.

They all sat back in silence, happy to rest and dream about more ice cream. Suddenly, to the left of them, one of Mr. Konkel's grandsons came running up.

"Look what Father bought me. Will you light it, Grandfather?" He held out a piece of metal shaped like a thin stick. It was thicker at one end, like a cattail.

Mr. Konkel struck a match and held it to the tip of the fatter end.

Ssss! Ssss! The stick began to crackle and sparks shot out in all directions.

"It's gunpowder! Jump out of the way!" shrieked Anna, remembering Jacob's accident two years ago.

"No," laughed Mr. Konkel. "It's only a bit of fireworks. A sparkler."

They watched as the sparks continued to zing out every which way, until at last the fat end of the metal stick was all burned off. That was the end of the fireworks.

"Too bad you didn't save it until after dark," said Mr. Konkel. "They shine much better then."

"Where did you buy it?" Mother asked the boy.

"At Bergaust's," he replied. "They've got lots more."

Mother looked questioningly at Father. Anna held her breath. Did that mean she wanted him to buy some of the sparkling sticks? Father hesitated, but then he seemed to change his mind.

"Well, I guess we can have a little foolishness now and then," he said. He reached into his pocket purse and gave some coins to Franciszek. "You can buy two or three with that, I should think. But we'll save them until dark, so bring them back here."

Anna was bursting with contentment. Just when she thought she had seen and heard everything connected with the Fourth of July, something new and exciting came along, like ice cream and sparklers.

"Mother, do they have Fourth of July in Poland?" she asked.

"Whatever do you want to know that for?" Mother's eyes opened wide.

"I want to know," insisted Anna.

"No. They don't have Fourth of July because this is an American holiday. Don't you remember? Father told you it was the birthday of America."

"If they don't celebrate the Fourth of July, then, do they have another birthday?"

"Not exactly," replied Mother. "But why do you ask such questions?"

"I want to go to Poland someday, but I'm not sure I'll like it if they don't have things like the Fourth of July."

"You won't get much celebrating in Poland, not under the Prussians," said Mr. Konkel.

"I'm not going to Prussia," Anna answered firmly. "They're too mean and strict there. I'm only going to Poland."

At that, Father and Mr. Konkel burst into laughter. Mother shook her head.

"Oh, Anna, don't you understand? If you go to our old home in Poland, you *have* to go to Prussia, because that part is under the Prussians now."

Anna did not understand.

"Then why do you always say you came from Poland? And you said you went *away* to the army, to Prussia," she told her father accusingly.

"I did, but that was still part of Poland. I mean, Prussia." Father looked at Mother helplessly. He did not seem to be able to word it clearly.

"We still call it Poland because we feel Polish, but the government is Prussian," explained Mother. "When they ordered everyone there to speak German, even in church, we didn't like that. Haven't you heard Father say, many times, that was one of the reasons we left to come here?"

Anna nodded, but she still did not understand completely.

"You mean there are no Polish kings and queens there?" she asked.

"No. Only Bismarck and the Kaiser," interrupted Father. "And I'm happy we left. We're under the American government here. We can speak Polish among ourselves if we want to, and have our church in Polish.

185

We're free to do what we want, and we can get free land, besides."

"You bet," added Mr. Konkel. "This is one hell of a free country." Then he cleared his throat because he could see Mother did not like such strong language. But Father was nodding his head and smiling.

"Those are my sentiments exactly," he agreed.

For the rest of that afternoon, Anna pondered what Mother and Father had said.

"I don't want to give up the Fourth of July," she thought. "And I don't want to go to Poland if it's not really Poland."

That evening, after supper and all the chores were done, they waited for it to get completely dark. Then Mother brought out the sparklers, and Father lit the tip of one. Taking turns, they waved the sparklers this way and that, making a fiery shower rain down from above. It was as though a million twinkly stars were falling over their farm.

Anna looked around at the shadowy forms of the house and barn. The outlines were so familiar, she would have recognized them anywhere, even in the deepest dark.

"I want to stay here," she thought. "Always." And this time the thought stayed with her even into her dreams.

Pronunciation Guide

PAGE 28
zocerka
zoh-tsair-kah

PAGE 57
pączki
ponch'-kee

PAGE 75
Sedzi sobie zając pod miedza,
seh-dzee soh-byeh zah-yontz pohd myeh-dzah
Pod miedza, pod miedza.
pohd myeh-dzah, pohd myeh-dzah
A myśliwy łedniem nie wiedzo,
ah meesh-lee-vee wed-nyem nyeh vyeh-dzoh
Nie wiedzo, nie wiedzo.
nyeh vyeh-dzoh, nyeh vyeh-dzoh

PAGE 78
Myszka
meesh-kah

PAGE 81
gvjozdki (gvjozdka)
gvyohzd'-kee (gvyohzd'-kah)

PAGE 82
Lulajże, Jezuniu, moja perełko,
lou-lye-zheh, yeh-zoo-nyou, moh-yah peh-rel-koh
Lulaj, ulubione me pieśidełko.
lou-lye, oo-lou-byoh'-neh meh pyesh'-chee-dil-koh
Lulajże, Jezuniu, lulajże, lulaj;

lou-lye-zheh, yeh-zoo-nyou, lou-lye-zheh, lou-lye
A ty go, Matuniu w płaczu utulaj.
ah tee goh, mah-too-nyou v pwa-choo oo-too'-lye

PAGE 99
kasha
kah'-shah

PAGE 106
Gazeta Polska
gah-zyet'-ah poll'-skah

PAGES 108, 109
"*'Gemeiner Pellowski. Kompagnie B. Dritte Bataillon.*
    (German)
geh-mine-erh pell-of-skee. kohm-pah-nee beh.
    drih-teh bah-tye-lyohn
Erstes Landwehr Regiment. Erste Infanterie Brigade.'"
    (German)
air-stess lahnd-vair reh-gee-ment. air-steh in-fahn-
    teh-ree brih-gah-deh

PAGE 111
Herr Kommandant (German)
hair kohm-mahn-dahnt'

PAGE 112
Herr Oberst (German)
hair oh'-burst

PAGE 137
Czarna ziemia, kamién biały,
char-nah zyem-yah, kah-myen byah-wee
Siedzi na nim Podolina.
seh-dzee nah neem pah-doh-leen-ah
Przyszedł do niej Podoleniec,
pshee-shedw doh nyey pah-doh-lee-nyets

"Podolanko, daj mi wieniec."
pah-doh-lahn-koh, dye mee vyey-nyets
Rada bym ci wieniec dała,
rah-dah bim chee vyey-nyets dah-wah
Gdybym brata się nie bojała."
gdee-bim brah-tah sheh nyeh boh-yah-wah

PAGE 138
"Otruj, brata rodzonego,
oh-truy, brah-tah roh-dzoh-neh-goh
Będziesz miała mnie samego."
ben-dzhiesh myah-wah mnyeh sah-meh-goh

PAGE 159
Dyngus
ding-oose

PAGE 160
Dyngus, Dyngus, po dwa jaja!
ding-oose, ding-oose poh dvah yah-yah
Nie chcę chleba tylko jaja!
nyeh khtseh hleh-bah till-koh yah-yah

PAGE 180
Jeszcze zespół dalej, jeszcze żywo dalej
yesh-cheh zess-poe dah-lay, yesh-cheh
   zhee-voh dah-lay
Jeszcze żywo dalej, na lewo.
yesh-cheh zhee-voh dah-lay, nah leh-voh
Jeszcze zespół dalej, jeszcze żywo dalej
yesh-cheh zess-poe dah-lay, yesh-cheh zhee-voh dah-
   lay
Jeszcze żywo dalej, na prawo.
yesh-cheh zhee-voh dah-lay, nah prah-voh

Family Tree

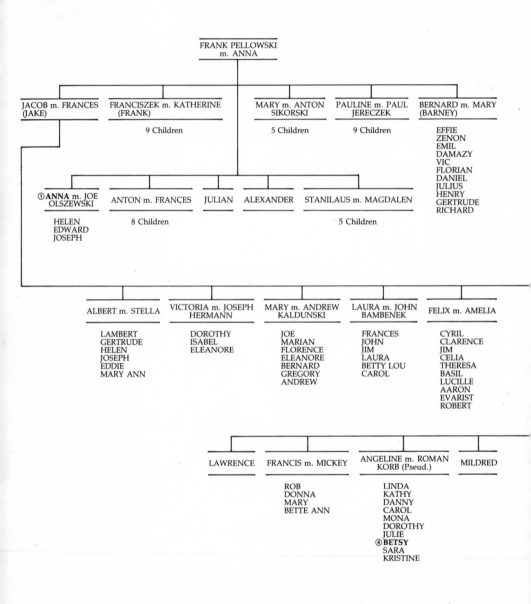

FRANK PELLOWSKI
m. ANNA

JACOB m. FRANCES
(JAKE)

FRANCISZEK m. KATHERINE
(FRANK)

9 Children

MARY m. ANTON
SIKORSKI

5 Children

PAULINE m. PAUL
JERECZEK

9 Children

BERNARD m. MARY
(BARNEY)

EFFIE
ZENON
EMIL
DAMAZY
VIC
FLORIAN
DANIEL
JULIUS
HENRY
GERTRUDE
RICHARD

①**ANNA** m. JOE
OLSZEWSKI

HELEN
EDWARD
JOSEPH

ANTON m. FRANCES

8 Children

JULIAN

ALEXANDER

STANILAUS m. MAGDALEN

5 Children

ALBERT m. STELLA

LAMBERT
GERTRUDE
HELEN
JOSEPH
EDDIE
MARY ANN

VICTORIA m. JOSEPH
HERMANN

DOROTHY
ISABEL
ELEANORE

MARY m. ANDREW
KALDUNSKI

JOE
MARIAN
FLORENCE
ELEANORE
BERNARD
GREGORY
ANDREW

LAURA m. JOHN
BAMBENEK

FRANCES
JOHN
JIM
LAURA
BETTY LOU
CAROL

FELIX m. AMELIA

CYRIL
CLARENCE
JIM
CELIA
THERESA
BASIL
LUCILLE
AARON
EVARIST
ROBERT

LAWRENCE

FRANCIS m. MICKEY

ROB
DONNA
MARY
BETTE ANN

ANGELINE m. ROMAN
KORB (Pseud.)

LINDA
KATHY
DANNY
CAROL
MONA
DOROTHY
JULIE
④**BETSY**
SARA
KRISTINE

MILDRED

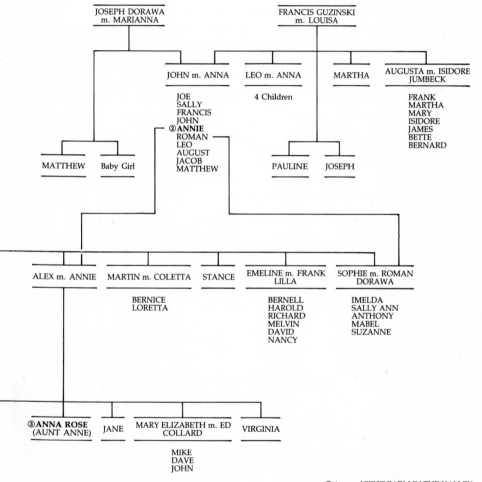

JOSEPH DORAWA
m. MARIANNA

FRANCIS GUZINSKI
m. LOUISA

JOHN m. ANNA

LEO m. ANNA

MARTHA

AUGUSTA m. ISIDORE
JUMBECK

JOE
SALLY
FRANCIS
JOHN
②ANNIE
ROMAN
LEO
AUGUST
JACOB
MATTHEW

4 Children

FRANK
MARTHA
MARY
ISIDORE
JAMES
BETTE
BERNARD

MATTHEW   Baby Girl

PAULINE   JOSEPH

ALEX m. ANNIE   MARTIN m. COLETTA   STANCE   EMELINE m. FRANK
LILLA   SOPHIE m. ROMAN
DORAWA

BERNICE
LORETTA

BERNELL
HAROLD
RICHARD
MELVIN
DAVID
NANCY

IMELDA
SALLY ANN
ANTHONY
MABEL
SUZANNE

③ANNA ROSE
(AUNT ANNE)   JANE   MARY ELIZABETH m. ED
COLLARD   VIRGINIA

MIKE
DAVE
JOHN

① Anna of FIRST FARM IN THE VALLEY.

② Annie of WINDING VALLEY FARM.

③ Anna Rose of STAIRSTEP FARM.

④ Betsy of WILLOW WIND FARM.

About the Author

ANNE PELLOWSKI was born in Pine Creek, Wisconsin. She is a graduate of the College of St. Teresa in Winona, Minnesota, and Columbia University, and has traveled widely throughout the world. A renowned storyteller and recognized authority on international literature as well as non-print media for children, Ms. Pellowski created and was for many years the Director of the Information Center for Children's Cultures of the United States Committee for UNICEF in New York City. At present, she is writing full time.

Based on the childhood experiences of Ms. Pellowski's great-aunt, *First Farm in the Valley: Anna's Story* is one of a quartet of books tracing four generations of a Polish-American family. *Winding Valley Farm: Annie's Story* recounts some of the experiences of Ms. Pellowski's mother; *Stairstep Farm: Anna Rose's Story* is based on the author's own childhood; and *Willow Wind Farm: Betsy's Story* on that of her sister Angie's daughter. *First Farm in the Valley* is chronologically the first of the books and Anna is the daughter of Frank, the original settler from Poland. There are more than 600 descendants of Frank Pellowski alive today, and this close-knit extended family provides a rich lode of material for Ms. Pellowski's future writing.

About the Artist

WENDY WATSON, daughter of a poet and an artist, grew up in a lively, creative family in Putney, Vermont. A graduate of Bryn Mawr College, she has illustrated more than fifty books for children, including *Jamie's Story* and *Has Winter Come?* (which she also wrote), and *Catch Me & Kiss Me & Say It Again*, a book of nursery rhymes written by her sister, Clyde. Miss Watson is the mother of two young children and lives in Toledo, Ohio.